THEO TURNED TO STARE AT HER.

For a moment, he allowed himself to be impressed, then his dislike of Ann reasserted itself and his lip curled slightly. "You seem to know a great deal about champagne, Miss Ingersoll. In general, I have found that men are superior judges of wine. Women tend to like anything that is sweet."

"*This* poor female does know a great deal about champagne. You might say it was in the blood," Ann responded sweetly. "And, I might add, I know horses." She was too angry to laugh at his deliberate goading. It was clear to her that he wanted her to find some excuse to leave him alone with Louisa. And it was becoming clear to him that she intended to remain firmly in place.

How dare she? he thought. No one ever gainsaid his wishes! He was a prince!

By Rebecca Baldwin

A LADY OF FASHION
A TANGLED WEB
A ROYAL VISIT

Published by HarperPaperbacks

A Royal Visit

A Regency Romance

⚞ REBECCA BALDWIN ⚟

HarperPaperbacks
A Division of HarperCollinsPublishers

🔥 HarperPaperbacks
A Division of HarperCollins*Publishers*
10 East 53rd Street, New York, N.Y. 10022-5299

This is a work of fiction. The characters, incidents, and
dialogues are products of the author's imagination and are not to
be construed as real. Any resemblance to actual events or
persons, living or dead, is entirely coincidental.

ISBN 0-06-108365-8

HarperCollins®, 🔥®, and HarperPaperbacks™, and
HarperMonogram®are trademarks of
HarperCollins*Publishers*, Inc.

Cover illustration by Jeff Barson

First HarperPaperbacks printing: December 1996

Printed in the United States of America

Visit HarperPaperbacks on the World Wide Web at
http://www.harpercollins.com/paperbacks

❖ 10 9 8 7 6 5 4 3 2 1

A Royal Visit

1

The view from the study was one of the most magnificent in the palace. From his desk, Prince Theodoric von Hazloe und Gottfreund could gaze out at the red tile rooftops and the rolling hills and beyond them, the glorious blue skies of a crisp autumn day. The hills above the valley were landscaped with lush vineyards, recently harvested of an abundant crop of grapes. Even as the prince gazed dreamily out the window, these grapes were being pressed into wine. Wine, no one needed to tell him, that would become the finest champagne in Europe. All the world knew about Batavian champagne, the lightest, driest, most sparkling celebration of the vintners' art in Europe. Champagne Batavia was not just the pride of the country; it was the basis of the entire economy.

But champagne was not what Theo was thinking about that afternoon as he gazed out the window, lost in his own thoughts.

A dark man with strong features, he might have been called handsome, had not hardship and experience set a cast to his face. At thirty-four, there were already shots of silver in his dark curls, and lines were incised between the curve of his lips and the edge of his nostrils. He had opened the neck of his uniform tunic, and the thin silver line of a scar, the memory of a bullet taken in an encounter with Bonaparte's troops, traced across his neck, disappearing into the dark curls of hair on his chest.

A slight breeze, with the edge of coming winter's chill in it, stirred the bulky parchments on his desk, and with an impatient exclamation, Prince Theo slapped his hand down on top of them, capturing them before they could fly away.

"Bored, dear cousin?" A languid voice asked from the depths of a capacious armchair by the ornately carved fireplace. Just the elegantly hosed and shod legs of this gentleman were visible, resting on an ottoman.

Theo grimaced. "You still here, Johannes?" he asked, keeping the irritation out of his voice.

In response, the gentleman in the chair leaned forward to look at the prince. Count Johannes von Hazloe's resemblance to his cousin was frequently remarked upon, although there could be no mistaking the two. Johannes was so handsome as to be almost pretty. Hardship had cut no lines into his smooth complexion, and his well-tended curls were unrelieved by gray. His gray eyes, so startling in one with his saturnine coloring, danced with amusement as he gazed upon his liege. "Where *should* I be, cousin?"

Johannes asked, picking an invisible speck of lint from his ceremonial uniform.

"In exile or on the block," Theo replied baldly.

With the sinuous grace of a cat, Johannes rose from the chair and bowed. "It would, of course, be my pleasure to die a martyr to my country," he said with the considerable sangfroid for which he was famous. He stretched. "But somehow, I think if you haven't disposed of me by now, you never will, dear cousin." Johannes crossed the room, going to a sideboard where he poured himself and his relative each a glass of Madeira. With an elegant gait, he traversed the Axminister rug and handed Theo his wine. "Don't worry, it's not poisoned," he said with his charming smile. "I would never want to usurp you when there are so many very dull and boring accounts to be gone over and details of budget and economy to be resolved. I know how to spend money, not make it."

Theo, accepting the glass, raised it in a mock salute. "Why is it," he sighed, "that no matter how much I ought to despise you, I can never quite bring myself to do so?"

"Because I am so charming of course," Johannes replied with simple pride. "Really, you know, it is my greatest gift."

"If it were not mingled with such a ridiculous jealousy of me," Theo said calmly, "perhaps I would appreciate it all the more. You know, cousin, you could work with me, not against me, for the good of the country."

"If it were not for an accident of birth, I would be Prince of Batavia and not you," Johannes sighed.

"And of course, I can *never* forgive you for that. I was brought up not to, you know. My father despised your father; it's a family tradition! Besides, you have to admit that I make life far more interesting for you than it would be without me."

Theo sighed. "Just be certain that you do not try to make it *too* interesting, lest you follow your father to the gallows," he said coldly.

"Treason? *Moi?*" Johannes asked in mock surprise. "Just for being the loyal opposition?" He clicked his tongue. "And I thought you believed in democratic reform! Whatever would your idol Mr. Jefferson say?"

"He would advise me to have you hung," Theo retorted. "And I will, if I ever catch you in any activity that jeopardizes the peace and well-being of this country. Good God, Jo, haven't we been through enough here in the past decade under Bonaparte?"

"Thus speaks a hero of the resistance," Johannes said lightly. "You know, not all of us are cut out to live the guerrilla life in the hills, running and hiding and playing at soldiering! So very exhausting, you know."

"We were hardly playing," Theo said grimly. "And precious little you did to aid us in deposing that fool of a Bonaparte cousin set up over the country! He almost ruined the vineyards with his ignorance!"

Johannes wagged a finger. "I was not a collaborator! I was merely pretending to be one so that I could gather information for the resistance. And I might add, I was quite useful. It would seem that I have a talent for espionage." He modestly examined his fingernails, then buffed them against the gold braid on his coat.

Theo was forced to admit to himself that this was true; Johannes had a remarkable talent for ferreting out secrets and gossip. A naturally inquisitive personality, combined with a talent for intrigue, made him useful. And although he might covet the Batavian crown for himself, he was far too much of a von Hazloe to enjoy seeing it on the head of someone outside the Family, especially if that someone had been a soapmaker from Ajaccio before his cousin Napoleon placed him on the puppet throne of a country no bigger than a lady's handkerchief.

Looking about himself at the hideous damask-papered walls and the grotesque changes the interloper's wife had created in the palace, Theo could not help but shudder. The Canova busts of Bonaparte had been removed, and the bees and initials picked out of the upholstery and the curtains, but there had been no money to spare to remove the ghastly empire moldings or the awful gilt furniture carved with lions' heads and alligator paws. Restoring the government and economy of the country had been a priority; from birth, Theo had been taught that the well-being of his subjects and the good of his country came before his own desires or comforts.

But Bonaparte had been on St. Helena for more than two years. Faced with the daunting task of rebuilding the looted wineries and restoring the damaged vineyards, Theo had barely had the time to think about anything other than the restoration of his country's peace and prosperity to prewar conditions. A fine harvest this year insured forthcoming prosperity and lifted an enormous burden from his shoulders.

It also gave him time to take a serious look at Johannes, which he was doing at that very moment.

His cousin had been admiring himself in the heavily-gilded mirror above the sideboard, but sensing Theo's thoughtful stare, he gave his epaulets one last adjustment and turned to face him.

"I don't like that expression," Johannes said warily. "When you look that particularly dark look at me, I just know that it means that I am going to be called to account for something I've done or you *think* I've done."

"No, it's what I think you're going to do," Theo replied. "And I am trying to decide what I ought to do with you. You'd like nothing better than to take my place, Jo, and I have a feeling you've been scheming to do it again."

Johannes bowed again. "If only I had your talent, your touch, shall I say, with the common people, then our situations would be reversed, you may depend upon it. Alas, I lack the popular support so necessary to the coup in a small country where everyone knows everyone else." He sighed regretfully.

Theo was about to say something else when the sound of church bells rang out. He glanced at the hideous ormolu clock on the mantel, another Bonaparte legacy.

"The Thanksgiving Service is about to start," Johannes said. "And if we are late, you know what the Archbishop will have to say to both of us. Dear cousin, you can't go out of the room like that," he added, tsking as he did up the buttons on the high collar of the prince's military tunic. Standing back to admire his work, Johannes shook his head. "If you are going to be a prince, you really ought to take more pains to look like one," he scolded.

Although he was profoundly grateful to the Deity for Batavia's deliverance and its bounteous harvest, Prince Theo sometimes found his attention wavering during the ancient Archbishop's interminable sermons. In a very small and very intimate place like Batavia, where everyone knew everyone else, he was fairly certain that there were others who felt the same way he did. He was hard put to suppress a smile when the snoring of the Captain of the Guards rose up from the pews, only to be stifled by the ministrations of that worthy's good wife. All the feathers on her bonnet shook indignation.

No matter what troubles he might have, Prince Theo reflected, at least he was not married. That, at least provided him with some comfort in the midst of all his burdens. There were times, he guiltily reflected, when he yearned to be back in the hills again, hiding in caves and foraging game in order to survive and strike out at Bonaparte's troops. Now, that, he thought, had been something more to his liking than this dreary round of ceremonial formality and endless seas of paperwork that seemed to swallow up his days. The last thing he needed or wanted these days was a wife, someone who would tie him down and tire him out with endless female—

"—and I know that I speak for everyone in Batavia when I say that the one thing we need and pray for is a princess who will provide us with an heir!" The Archbishop finished in ringing tones.

Although he was far too well trained to jerk bolt upright in his pew, Theo's eyes widened and his hands clenched at the prayer book in his lap at these words. A look of panic almost—but not quite— passed over his features.

"That's right!" murmured a parishioner some-where, and there were murmurs of assent throughout the congregation, even a smattering of applause.

"A princess! An heir!"

"Prince Theo must marry!"

"Theodoric must give us a successor!"

Johannes, sitting beside him smiled a very wicked smile. "Being a hero is never enough, as you see," he murmured, enjoying his cousin's discomfort.

Theo cast a glance around the vaulted cathedral. The eyes of the entire congregation were on him, and they were beaming at him in expectation.

"Rise and speak to your people!" The Archbishop commanded him benevolently.

It is hard to resist the importuning of a man who has known you since infancy. Running a finger around suddenly too-tight collar of his tunic, the prince rose to his feet and turned to the congregation. "I am, er, aware of my duty, and I promise that I shall do my best to fulfill my, er, domestic obligations. If Batavia wants a princess, then I shall marry. As soon as I can find a suitable wife," he added.

Almost the entire population of Batavia was present,

and the roar of approval that issued from their throats must have awakened the ancient knights sleeping in their tombs along the walls. Madam Desfontes, the ancient organist, struck up the national anthem, and Prince Theodoric found himself being hoisted on the shoulders of the men who had served under him in the wars. As he was carried on their shoulders from the church to the waiting feast tables in the open square, four hundred patriotic souls cheered for their beloved prince.

"Let the Thanksgiving feast begin!" the archbishop commanded.

Only Johannes, his eyes guarded and his fingers locked tightly around his prayer book, remained behind, staring thoughtfully at nothing, while the music swirled up and around his head.

It was past dark when Theo, feeling over full of wine and food, staggered into his palace bedchamber. His valet was still at the celebrations, but a low lamp burned on the bedside stand and his nightclothes were laid out on a chair. Like most of the private rooms in the palace, his bedchamber was nearly bare; the retreating Bonaparte cousin and his wife had managed to carry away nearly everything of value. Used to Spartan conditions, Theo barely noticed.

The distant sound of music and laughter floated through the open windows as he unbuttoned his tunic and threw it carelessly on a chair. He sighed with relief to be freed of its confines, for he had grown to dislike uniforms very much in the past few years.

He walked across the room to the washstand, pouring water from the pitcher into the bowl and taking up a bar of soap to wash his face and hands. As he looked into the small mirror above the washstand, he thought he saw a movement in the dark shadows of the room.

With the iron control born of soldiering, he forced himself not to betray his surprise, but rather picked up the straight razor on the washstand, pretending to prepare himself to shave as he watched the shadows, trying to determine if it was the flicker of the lamplight or something more sinister.

A human form moved in the shadows, coming toward him. With lightning speed, Theo turned, brandishing the razor, stanced to fight.

"I say, H. M.," said a voice in the distinct accents of the English. "That's hardly the way to treat an old friend, don't you know!"

A tall blond man attired in travel stained clothes moved into the light, grinning at the prince.

With a most unprincely whoop of joy, Theo cast the razor down and opened his arms. The Englishman opened his also and the two men caught each other in an embrace. "Good God, man!" Theo cried after many manly back poundings, "You're loosing your touch! I saw you in the shadows!"

Colonel Randolph Rodney, late of His Majesty's 21st, stood back to have a better look at his friend. "Peace has put us both out of practice," he laughed. "Two years ago, you would have cut my throat and asked questions later! How are you, Prince? By God, you look grand!"

"And so do you, although I would have been hard-pressed to recognize you in your civilian dress! Lord, we've become quite the Corinthian, haven't we?"

"Forgive my dirt. I arrived too late to meet you at the Cathedral—my carriage broke down at Calais—so I thought that I would surprise you, for old times' sake! Like I did at Schloss Bembreck that night when old le Clerc had you cornered," the colonel chuckled. He was a few years older than the prince, of a heavier build and a more choleric complexion. His blue eyes danced as he looked at his old companion in arms.

"And I tell you, we could have fought our way out of that one! But we were damned glad to have the help cleaning up." Theo pounded his old friend on the back. "Brandy is what we both need, to drink a toast to the old days—and another to the future!"

"I wouldn't say no," Randolph replied. "Sneaking around palaces is thirsty work. Your guard leaves something to be desired, you know."

Theo, removing a bottle of Batavian brandy from a sideboard, shrugged. "There's a celebration tonight. Everyone is down there, including my cousin Johannes." He poured two glasses, handing one to the colonel.

"Ah, he's still around, hey?" Randolph said in neutral tones.

"And still very, very ambitious. But I think he's been declawed. The war, you know, took a great deal out of him. As it did all of us."

"Ah," Randolph said. He frowned. "If he weren't your cousin, Prince, I think I would tell you to dispose of him. His kind is dangerous."

"His tongue, I think, is more dangerous than anything else about him. Insurrection takes effort. And Johannes is the laziest man I know," Theo replied lightly. He refilled his friend's glass.

"Hmm," the colonel said. He looked as if he would like to say more, but kept his silence.

They sat on opposite sides of the fire and drank their brandy. "I had nearly forgotten," Randolph said thoughtfully, holding his glass to the light, "how smooth, how fair your wines are in this country. In England, now, there's a market for this sort of vintage."

"I am thinking that we must start expanding our markets," Theo said. "In fact, you would be surprised at what a dull dog I have become, all business and accounts, just like a merchant. Which is in a sense what I am. It's my job to make sure Champagne Batavia graces every elegant table in Europe."

The conversation drifted into other days and other times, which, seen through the hazy golden glow of time and victory, took on a very romantic aura indeed. At the time it was happening the war had been terrifying, ugly, and often bloody. Looking backward through the haze of very good brandy, it seemed to have been one of the most exciting events in their lives. As the brandy bottle emptied, the prince and the colonel waxed very nostalgic indeed.

"What happened to that dark-haired gal up in St. Micral?" Randolph asked. "Now she was a proper armful!"

Theo sighed sentimentally, shrugging. "Married a blacksmith, I believe. When you're responsible to everyone, you know, you don't get to see much of the females. At least not in a principality where everyone knows you and you know everyone. If you as much as *talk* to a pretty girl, everyone gossips about it for weeks afterward."

"Batavia is like an English village in that way," the colonel laughed. "But you must admit that it helped us a great deal when we were fighting the French. Our best intelligence network was the population at large."

"And we were grateful to England for sending your forces to help us," the prince acknowledged. "I only wish you could help me now, Randolph!"

"Say the word, and you have my aid, Prince!" Randolph promised in a glow of brandy.

"They want me to get married. To provide an heir and all of that."

Theo looked so woebegone that the colonel burst into laughter. "Leg-shackled, hey? Once again, I thank my lucky stars that I am not you!"

"I must, of course, bow to the will of the people," Theo said gloomily, stretching out his legs, propping his feet on the fender. "And besides, got to have an heir! The idea of Johannes inheriting makes my blood curdle. But—" he passed a hand through his dark silvered curls, "I'd like to have some enjoyment out of life before I've got to settle down."

"You *have* become a dull dog," the colonel agreed. "Not havin' any pleasure in life at all! When is the last time you went hunting or had a game of cards or a race or even a mill?"

Theo shook his head. "I can't remember," he

said. "There's been so much to set to rights that I haven't had the time to do much else but look at accounts, hold meetings, and worry about mold on the grapes. We almost had to start all over again, you know. Batavia took quite a battering in the war."

To this, Colonel Rodney had to agree. The two men gazed thoughtfully into the fire for a second.

"The thing is," the prince said after a moment's reflection, "princesses aren't all that easy to come by these days. Either they're the wrong religion or they're not interested in a poor country like Batavia. Actually, Batavia is flush again, thanks to the harvest this year; it's the von Hazloe fortunes that are sadly depleted."

Colonel Rodney was too polite to comment on this, but he cast a look about the shabby chamber. The royal family's personal fortunes, he knew, had never been large. But the Bonaparte cousin had managed to deplete what he could before absconding in the middle of the night with a wagon train of loot. "One solution." He coughed discreetly. "Marry an heiress."

Theo smiled. "What heiress would have me? None of the great families of Europe are anxious to tie their fortunes to a tiny principality in the middle of nowhere, you know."

"Must the lady be of royal blood?" Colonel Rodney asked thoughtfully.

Theo shook his head ruefully. "That would seem out of the question. My mother, as you know, was of an excellent family, but not royal, so there is no tradition of intermarriage. Choosing a female from Batavia is out of the question, too; they're nearly all my cousins by blood or marriage. Besides, known them all since I was in leading strings; it would be like marrying a sister." He thoughtfully swallowed a mouthful of brandy. "In my position, you don't marry for love, I've known that since I was a child. It's my duty to marry to further Batavian interests here and abroad. All I can hope for is that she won't be too ugly or too stupid. But I'd best do it soon. All I heard today was that it's my duty to marry and produce an heir!" He shuddered. "And I have a very strong feeling that if I don't come up with a suitable female soon, the Archbishop and the Chancellor will find someone for me. Some doughy German princess with a squint and a dowry!"

Both men sat in contemplative silence for several moments.

Colonel Rodney sat up straight. "By Jove, Prince, I believe I've got it! An Englishwoman!"

"Where?" Theo asked, looking around as if he expected to see Britannia herself emerge from the shadows.

"Marry an Englishwoman! Nothing to it! Right religion, more or less, strong ties to commerce, a tidy personal fortune! It shouldn't be too hard for you, you know! You did go to Oxford, your English is good, better than my French or German, you're a decent enough lookin' fella, and from what I've seen, you know how to address the ladies in the language they like! Show up now, cause a stir in the London Season! Daresay Town is full of heiresses who would like nothing better than to be a royal princess! And when you think about that lot they've got at home, Prinny's brothers, why you're above a prize! Young, handsome, a war hero with his own kingdom, well, it just goes to show you! Besides, you're dashed good ton! Everyone says so! "

"You're mad, Randolph," Theo said when he was able to stop laughing long enough.

"Not at all, old boy! Nothing wrong with my upper works! In fact, I think I may know the very lady. M'cousin, Lady Louisa Coldstone! Old Coldstone's eldest daughter. A damned fine looking gal, too; in fact she's an acknowledged beauty. In the blond way, you know, with a neat figure, and a handsome chunk of personal fortune to be hers! And believe me, the Dukes of Coldstone already fancy themselves better than the Royals, which if you look at their pedigree, they are. Louisa's been brought up to conduct herself like Royalty. She'd make a fine princess, don't you know!" Waxing rhapsodic, Colonel Rodney mentioned a six figure annuity.

Theo laughed. "Lead me to her!" he said.

"No, oh no old man, I am serious! Dead serious," the colonel said. "Lady Louisa is the gal for you, think on it! There's nothing old Coldstone would like better than to see his daughter a royal princess, you see. Damned proud family. And she's well educated, too. Speaks three languages, reads Latin, too. Wouldn't have to train her up, either; she'd be able to step right into her role. Anyone who's grown up at Coldstone Castle as the daughter of a Public Man like the Duke will know just how to go on as Princess von Hazloe!" The colonel beamed at his friend through a brandy mist. "If anything, the Coldstones are much grander than the von Hazloes," he added ingenuously.

"You frighten me," Theo teased his old friend. He rose from his chair and paced the length of the chamber, pausing to look out the window at the feast, still continuing in the square below. Not for the first time, he felt a sense of entrapment in his position and his palace.

It had been more than a decade since he had been at university in Oxford, but he recalled the country and his student days with a great affection. He had always had an affinity for the English, and for English ladies. Certainly, he could do worse than select a bride from a country that, with the end of the long wars, was beginning to dominate world commerce. Such an alliance would strengthen the trade agreements he was hoping to make with Britain, whose ships sailed all over the world. Ships that could carry the champagnes of his landlocked country to wine lovers everywhere. Batavian champagne could compete with the wines of France, if only people knew about its excellent quality!

His thoughts turned again to the gray stone buildings and the tall spires of Oxford, making him nostalgic for his carefree student days, for a time when the heavy weight of responsibility had rested on his father's shoulders, rather than his. Sentiment combined with excellent brandy to cloud his head. But still, why not? He knew that sooner or later, he must make a state visit to England, to talk trade and commerce and treaties. Why not combine it with a look at Lady Louisa Coldstone?

"By Gad, Randolph, I'll do it!" he exclaimed, turning away from the window.

"Eh?" Randolph asked, startled out of his own reveries. The brandy bottle nearly slipped from his hand.

"I'll go back to England with you! I'll look among the English roses for a princess! Yes! That is what I will do!" Theo proclaimed.

He ruined the effect of this only a little by staggering into a nearby chair. "Yes! That may well be the solution to everything. Besides, I need a holiday. Haven't had one in two years, you know. Combine work with pleasure!"

"That's a grand scheme, Prince, old chap!" the colonel said. "Have a little more brandy to toast it."

"Don't mind if I do!" Theo replied. "Daresay after I am leg-shackled, having any sort of a turn-up at all will be out of the question! To England and a wife!"

Outside the closed door of his bedchamber, the sound of two glasses clashing in a toast made a lurking figure wince.

Johannes, Count von Hazloe, who had been doing what he did best, listening at keyholes, winced.

"To England and a wife indeed!" he hissed under his breath. "Oh, no, my dear cousin, no heirs for you! No brats to place me one more step away from the throne if I can help it!"

2

It was commonly accepted that the Dukes of Coldstone were wont to live in a style as grand or even grander than the Royal Family. Although the Coldstones were far too well-bred to mention it, their lineage was far older, their holdings far more vast than those of the mere German upstarts on the throne. In *Burke's Peerage*, the family's origins were "lost in the mists of antiquity" and the incumbent's various titles so ancient that the present duke was the twenty-second in his line. Each succeeding duke had added considerably to the family's fortunes and holdings through sound management and fortuitous marriage, with the happy result that the present titleholder was one of the richest men in Europe. His heir, the Earl of Seabright, could reasonably be expected to multiply his inheritance in his lifetime. Indeed, he had already proved himself a true Coldstone by making an advantageous marriage with an heiress who had promptly produced two sturdy young sons and was expecting a third child in the winter, thus insuring the succession would march on into the new century unimpaired.

Neither the duke nor his duchess had cause for complaint in their eldest daughter, Louisa. Now in her second season, Lady Louisa Coldstone was an acknowledged beauty, a cool and elegant blonde. While her fortune and family assured that she did not lack for suitors, her comeliness assured that she was one of the most sought-after females in the Upper Ten Thousand.

Known to the rejected hopefuls who had sought her hand as Ice, Lady Louisa presented a deceptively cool face toward the world. Raised in the strictest propriety, she combined a pink-and-white perfection of feature and figure with the formal manner that seemed to be a Coldstone family trait. Two years spent at Miss Ridgely's Seminary, that most exclusive and exacting female finishing academy in Bath, had added regal posture and rigid deportment to her talents, while deploying a rather ceremonious aspect to a character formed from birth to be a Coldstone. For the family, to be a Coldstone was all. In due course, it would be her obligation to marry in a way that would advance the family, but for now her parents were content to enjoy the social success of their eldest daughter, whose heart remained unmoved.

"For you may be sure, Louisa, that there is nothing gentlemen like so much as the appearance of a female who is unattainable," her best friend Miss Ingersoll reassured her.

For those who said that Lady Louisa Coldstone was too grand by far and too aware of her own consequence, her friendship with Ann Ingersoll was something of a puzzle. Miss Ingersoll was after all, the daughter of a Cit, a wine merchant who made no bones about his humble origins or the success of his own endeavors to raise a enormous fortune in trade. No one could have predicted that these two damsels would form a fast friendship at Miss Ridgely's, or that their friendship would survive their emergence from the school into two very different worlds. And yet, there they were, seated in the yellow Morning Room at Coldstone House, their heads together, reading the letter Lady Louisa had received from her cousin Randolph.

Those who had been privileged to visit Coldstone Castle, the ancestral estate in the Cotswolds, or Coldstone House, the ducal mansion in Grosvenor Square, were often intimidated by the vaulted rooms and grandiose trappings of an ancient and distinguished family. The Dukes, Public Men all, had furnished their principal residences with due thought for the ceremonies and entertainments that were a part of their various offices and responsibilities. Even the London house's Morning Room, pronounced "warm" and "cozy" by the family, was a large vaulted and carved chamber with a fireplace large enough that four men could stand erect inside the hearth. Miss Ingersoll was not among those so easily intimidated. However, she did drawl her shawl closer about her shoulders, since the small coal fire in the grate did very little to warm the vast chamber in the damp and rainy afternoon. The Coldstones were firm believers that warm rooms were a sign of lassitude; cool rooms were considered invigorating, even in the most Arctic weather.

"'The Prince, I think, is a handsome man, and not quite in the common style, and his manners are such as must please, civil and always amiable as he is. I think that the London ladies will find him attractive company . . .'" Ann read aloud in her low voice. She looked up at her friend, her gray eyes dancing. "He sounds like the prince in a fairy tale," she remarked.

"I think that the description of His Highness is meant to intrigue us," Lady Louisa replied gravely.

"Intrigue *you*, perhaps. As for me, I can't imagine anyone less interesting than a prince. A bit above my touch, but perfect for you!"

She was rewarded with one of Louisa's rare sunny smiles. "I wish Mama could hear you say so! It seems my parents feel no one is good enough for a Coldstone. Save perhaps a prince or one of the Royal Dukes!"

"No, I thank you! Not one of the Regent's brothers!" Anne screwed up her face. "Not only are they all quite old, but *such* loose fish!"

"Quite a dreadful expression, but alas, all too true, much to Mama and Papa's disappointment." Louisa said. "Oh, Ann, I think that Miss Ridgely would be less than proud of the way I have forsaken Miss Wollstonecraft's ideas, the principles of women's rights she tried so hard to instill in us!"

Thinking of their former preceptress, Miss Ingersoll nodded. "I fear that there is much that we have learned in theory that we are unable to put into practice in reality." Her tone was slightly bitter. "Feminist principles are all very well, and we must do all that we can to insure that women attain the same rights as men, but it is not easy!"

"Especially for me," Lady Louisa murmured gloomily. "I must marry, you know; for me there can be no other choice." She sighed. "I wish I were like you, Ann, determined to remain single and to further the cause of women's rights."

"Hush!" Ann replied, only half in jest. "If anyone knew what bluestocking principles we cherish, you may be sure that every effort would be made to sever our friendship! You don't think my father has changed his mind about women since the last time you saw him, do you?"

"No, probably not! But why must marriage be the only career open to a female? Why is it that men will persist in viewing women as inferior creatures? Why must we marry if we wish to have any life at all? And why cannot I marry for love? How lucky you are to determine that you shall always remain single and have the expectations to allow you to do so."

"Yes, I suppose so, but if you think my father has not thrust a great many men in my path, then you don't know him as well as I think you do! But I am determined never to allow myself to succumb to such a foolish emotion as love."

"That is because you have never met someone who could make you feel the way love makes you feel," Louisa said. "It is quite a separate thing from one's principles. Why, even Miss Wollstonecraft married Mr. Godwin!"

"I am not likely to find my Mr. Godwin, situated as I am. Besides, beneath your cool exterior there is a great deal of passion! *I* am as cold as ice, I swear! Besides, dear Louisa, you don't lack for suitors, even if none of them are royal," Ann replied practically, looking about the room. It seemed as if every available surface was filled with bouquets, tokens of esteem from Lady Louisa's many admirers. "Sometimes when I come to visit you, it smells as if there's been a death in the family. And more arrive as we've been sitting here!"

Lady Louisa surveyed the floral tributes without enthusiasm.

"Yes, I suppose it is flattering," she murmured. "If one cared a jot about any of them!"

"Still not in love?" Ann asked.

"Not a bit," Louisa admitted. "It is driving Mama quite mad. I think she thinks that I should at least feel a certain *tendre* for someone, anyone, even if he's totally ineligible."

"Sir Gervais Mordaunt?

"No."

"Lord Westerbrook?"

"No."

"Mr. Quigley?"

"Heavens, no!" Louisa shook her head vehemently. "Ann, he *spits* when he talks!"

"An anathema to romance, to be sure," Ann said dryly. "Well, then, I suppose it will have to be this foreign prince. Well, Louisa, it is to be hoped he is better than one of the domestic variety."

"Heaven forfend! No woman should be forced to

marry one of the Royal Dukes! What a thoroughly
ramshackle set, besides all of them being quite, as you
say, loose fish!" Louisa smiled her little smile and
shook her head. "No, I am afraid that in my position,
love is out of the question. Coldstones don't marry
for love, Ann. They marry to further the family interests." She shrugged. "So, it might as well be this
Batavian prince as anyone, don't you think?" She leveled a blue-eyed gaze at her friend.

Ann sighed. "It's still Randolph, isn't it?" she
asked shrewdly.

Louisa threaded the fringes of her shawl through
her fingers. A faint rosy blush, the only sign of her
discomfort, appeared in her cheeks.

"Oh, Louisa, I am sorry," Ann said sincerely. Lady
Louisa was not one to wear her heart upon her sleeve,
and indeed rarely spoke of her feelings. Emotions, it
would seem, were unseemly for a daughter of
Coldstone. Ann would have pursued this clue, but her
friend turned it away.

"It doesn't matter!" Lady Louisa replied briskly.
"You know, Ann, that Papa would never allow me to
marry a man who doesn't have the least consequence
in the world! Besides, Randolph doesn't have the
faintest idea—doubtless he still thinks of me as his
little cousin twice removed! Heaven forbid anyone
but you should know!"

Ann was about to say that she thought Louisa very
poor spirited indeed if she could allow the great love
of her life to escape so easily. However, at that
moment, Louisa's mama walked into the room and the
conversation abruptly switched directions.

Her Grace, the Duchess of Coldstone, had borne her duke five pledges of her affection over the years, yet she still retained the frosty beauty she had passed on her daughter. As Ann rose to her feet to greet her friend's mama, the duchess smiled, for she was fond of Miss Ingersoll, in spite of her indifferent pedigree. True, if Ann had been a great beauty, or even fair enough to compete with Louisa's blonde and creamy coloring, her feelings might be different.

As it was, she had been wary when her eldest daughter, usually so aware of what was due the Family, had struck up a friendship with a girl whose origins were, frankly, a little common. However, Ann Ingersoll's manners were perfectly genteel. Her tradesman father, while sometimes referred to, was rarely seen. Her worst suspicion, that Mr. Ingersoll might attempt to use Ann's friendship with Lady Louisa to push his daughter or himself forward into the upper reaches of Society that the Coldstones occupied, never materialized. Hard as she found it to credit, Mr. Ingersoll, a widower of some years' standing, seemed indifferent to the ways of the Upper Ten Thousand. The duke, who dined with him at his club from time to time, pronounced him a man of superior understanding, and profited from Mr. Ingersoll's business advice.

Her Grace suspected, but was never able to prove to herself, that Miss Ingersoll's worst fault was a certain irreverent sense of humor. Lacking in that gift herself, Her Grace naturally deplored it in others. But she was not an unkind woman, and had to admit that Ann was very ladylike, a well-mannered girl without any hint of vulgarity or taint of the shop about her. And she seemed to have a good influence on Louisa. Of a consequence, the duchess had unbent enough to allow Louisa to include Ann in most of her entertainments.

"Dearest Ann! It is excessively kind of you to come and bear Louisa company today," she said, bidding the girls resume their seats. "She's been a trifle out of sorts of late, haven't you dear?" The duchess touched her daughter's shoulder.

"I'm *fine*, Mama," Lady Louisa said in the world-weary way of daughters everywhere.

"I see you are sharing Randolph's letter with Ann, my dear. The prince was made known to us when the duke was in Vienna. A very gentlemanly man, we thought. And a hero in the war! We certainly look forward to having him visit us." The duchess's voice was just a little too bright, and over Louisa's head, she cast Ann what would have been a pleading look from a lesser being.

"He sounds very appealing," Ann replied dutifully. She handed the letter to the duchess. "I am sure that Colonel Rodney does not exaggerate his virtues."

Her Grace nodded gratefully. "He shall arrive within the week, I think. Goodness, there will be a great deal to attend to. I think we should have a ball in his honor, don't you, my dear?"

"Just as you wish, Mama," Lady Louisa replied colorlessly.

Her Grace shot her daughter a sharp look. "Louisa, just once I wish that you would show some enthusiasm for some gentleman," she sighed. "Your father and I have done everything within our power to put you in the way of meeting the right sort of gentleman. With Jane coming up from the schoolroom next year, my dear, and so many men at your feet, I would have hoped—"

Ann, seeing the blush in Louisa's cheeks deepen, quickly diverted the duchess's attention by asking after the health of the duke, her children, and especially her grandchildren. Since these last named were always a favorite subject, Her Grace was happy to share the latest doings of little Gerald and Charles with Miss Ingersoll, who listened with the appearance of far more interest than she was feeling.

Thus, nothing more was said at that moment about the forthcoming royal visit, but when Miss Ingersoll took her leave, she pressed her friend to visit her in Berkeley Square very soon. Unspoken was their mutual determination to speculate further upon this matter.

"Papa, what do you know about Batavia?" Ann asked. "I very much think that the Coldstones believe only a prince will do for poor Louisa," she informed her father over the dinner table that night. "So they have set their hearts on the Prince of Batavia." The two of them were dining *en famile* in Berkeley Square that evening. While Mr. Ingersoll's home was no rival for the palatial grandeur of Coldstone House, it was no mere town house either, but a handsomely apportioned Palladian dwelling whose interiors reflected an eye for the modern in both design and comfort. Mr.

Ingersoll was a great believer in progress. As the most successful wine broker in London, he had the financial wherewithal to indulge himself in such modern innovations as gas lighting, central heating, and interior plumbing, and the foresight to invest heavily in these, the coming things. The result was that Mr. Ingersoll's home was far warmer and better illuminated than Coldstone House. "I think they mean that Louisa should make a match with this prince, sight unseen. After all, Jane is pushing to get out of the schoolroom now, and Catherine is right behind her, so how long can the duchess continue to allow Louisa to go unmarried?"

Mr. David Ingersoll, every inch the successful and prosperous businessman, who had been savoring his dinner and thinking about the problems of an inferior shipment of hock now lying in his warehouses at Wapping, recalled himself with a small start. "How's that?" he asked, looking fondly upon his only daughter. "Lady Louisa, you say?"

Ann smiled at her father. "Batavia, Papa. What do you know about Batavia?"

"Best champagne in Europe. Dry, good legs, just a fruity breath, deep color, full body," Mr. Ingersoll offered. "But you can find all that out for yourself. The Prince of Batavia is coming to visit England. Part of his mission is to flog his country's champagne, so I daresay you can meet him if you're interested. I shall certainly be speaking with him about getting the license to export Champagne Batavia through Ingersoll Limited." Enlightenment dawned on his dark, thin face. "You don't mean to tell me that the duchess is planning to throw Lady Louisa at the prince, do you?" he asked.

"It would certainly appear that way," Ann said thoughtfully. "You know she must make a good marriage, but a foreign prince—well, I imagine he's dull and stuffy and has a Hapsburg jaw or worse."

Mr. Ingersoll could have said that Lady Louisa was a trifle dull and stuffy herself, had anyone asked his opinion. Unlike the Coldstones, the origins of the Ingersolls were not lost in the mists of antiquity, but written carefully down in the parish registers of the City and the ledgers of Ingersoll Limited for many generations. The Ingersolls had been wine and spirits merchants for as many generations back as anyone cared to remember, their business rising steadily in the world, generation after generation, until Mr. David Ingersoll had inherited the business, seen its great possibilities, and begun to expand the company until it dominated the trade, and not inconsequentially, made Mr. Ingersoll one of the richest men in England. As proud as the Coldstones were of their lineage, Mr. Ingersoll was proud of his. Reflecting upon the information imparted by his daughter, he thought for a moment.

Mr. Ingersoll shrugged. "Just don't let me see you swooning for the fella! Remember, you were reared on democratic principles! When I think of all the time and money spent to educate you, my girl, I hate to see it thrown away on some European ne'er-do-well who inherited everything he owns."

"Papa, really!" Ann responded indignantly. "You

think I would be interested in the Prince of Batavia? I don't even know the man!"

Mr. Ingersoll smiled at his daughter, thinking how very like her late mother she was. Although she was not a great beauty like Lady Louisa, she was by far more lively. Her nut-brown hair curled appealingly around a heart-shaped face highlighted by a speaking pair of gray eyes, and her small mouth was drawn by nature into an appealing upward curve. Slightly above the medium height, she was a gracefully built, fine-boned young woman with an olive complexion that betrayed just a hint of rose beneath her skin. Her father had every reason to be proud of his daughter. Her understanding was superior and she was possessed of a fine common sense. Although he was fond of Lady Louisa, he sometimes worried that her family's fashionable ways might lead his daughter astray from the sound principles upon which she had been reared. He had spent a great deal of time and money ensuring that his daughter received the finest upbringing and education available to a female. She had returned home, not as he had feared, stuffed full of grand ideas about her station in life, but, to his mind, more puzzling, with the strange idea that females should have the same rights as men! Liberal though Mr. Ingersoll might be in his politics, this idea was thoroughly alien to him, and nothing his daughter could do or say would change his mind.

Happily for the peace of the household, following several heated debates, father and daughter had tacitly agreed to disagree on this subject. "Is this why I paid out a small ransom to that woman?" Mr.

Ingersoll would complain at the end of each debate. "I wanted you to get a good education, not have your head stuffed full of radical notions!"

It was Mr. Ingersoll's profound hope that a return to the paternal residence would restore his daughter to her former sanity. For her part, Ann had decided that her father was hopelessly, stuffily Gothic, and therefore beyond reason.

Wisely, she had not presented him with her decision to remain single, or he would have been carried off by a fit of apoplexy. Devoted as she was to her views on female emancipation, she was also extremely fond of her parent, and wished him to live for many more years in good health.

As a man who had inherited a small wine shop and parlayed it into the largest and most prosperous brokerage in the kingdom, he was well aware that the stigma of a parent in Trade would always bar his daughter from the highest reaches of the ton. Like many businessmen, he distrusted the residents of the Fashionable World and its decadent enticements and code of inherited wealth. Like the Coldstones, he had had concerns about the suitability of Ann and Louisa's friendship, and for much the same reasons. Fortunately, he had found nothing objectionable about Lady Louisa, and even overcome his prejudices against Society enough to enjoy a casual friendship with the duke, whom he found to be a reasonable enough fellow, for a member of the decadent peerage. They shared a common problem in their daughters.

Ann had left school two years ago, and had displayed no inclination to form an attachment to a suitable, or even unsuitable gentleman. She seemed perfectly content to manage her father's household, to go hither and yon with her friends, to pursue her own interests without any particular consideration for marriage. And forward thinking as Mr. Ingersoll might be, he was still old-fashioned enough to wish to see his daughter comfortably settled. With this thought in mind, he glanced at the clock on the mantelpiece and frowned slightly.

"Don't you like the roast, Papa?" Ann asked. "I particularly asked Cook to keep it rare for you," she reminded him, misinterpreting the expression on her father's face.

"Oh, no, no, everything is just as it should be," Mr. Ingersoll said quickly. "It's just that I expected young Briggs with some bills of lading. It's that hock, you know. Espil sent us twenty cases of swill, not wine, and it must be dealt with immediately."

"Oh. Mr. Briggs," Ann said without enthusiasm. "Should I tell Addle to show him into your office when he comes?"

"No, no, I've given instructions to have him shown directly in when he comes. Fine young man, Jeremy Briggs." He dabbed at his lips with his napkin, watching his daughter warily.

"Don't you think so?" he asked when Ann did not immediately reply.

"Yes," she said tonelessly. "I am sure that Mr. Briggs is totally unexceptional."

As if taking this as his cue, Addle, the Ingersoll butler, opened the dining room doors and, in majestic tones, announced: "Mr. Briggs, sir!"

Ann shot her father a sharp look, but Mr. Ingersoll avoided her eye as he beckoned his assistant into the room with a hearty greeting.

Jeremy Briggs, aged twenty-four, but appearing somewhere between fifty and death, entered the room bearing before him a portfolio case. He was tall and thin as a clothes pole and cadaverous in appearance. Only the extreme whiteness of his shirt and stock set off the funereal black of his clothes. When he smiled, he exposed a set of large, vulpine teeth.

"Good evening, Miss Ann—sir!" he announced in his sepulchral tones. As he bowed, Ann looked at his thin frame and dark raiment with distaste. As usual when she beheld Mr. Briggs, she wondered if his hairline could recede any further without sliding off his head entirely.

"Mr. Ingersoll, I have the invoices you requested. I have taken the liberty of drafting a response to Señor Espil's letter of the 29th March, and—"

"Yes, yes, my boy, I see that you have," Mr. Ingersoll said, fitting his spectacles over his ears and gesturing toward the portfolio. "I'll take a look at that, if you please! Ann, perhaps young Briggs would like a cup of coffee or a bit of dinner."

"Please sit down, Mr. Briggs," Ann said civilly, if not enthusiastically. "Have you eaten yet?"

"Oh, yes, I supped on a lonely bachelor's meal in my lodgings. But a cup of coffee from your sweet hands, Miss Ann, now that would be a treat!" He rubbed his hands together, nodding his head.

Mr. Ingersoll took the portfolio and withdrew from the conversation, plunging himself into mass of

papers, harumphing and shaking his head. Miss
Ingersoll was left to entertain Mr. Briggs, who settled
into a chair at the table in the same way a spider
settles into its web.

"I see I find you well, dear Miss Ann," Mr. Briggs
said, gazing at her with colorless eyes from a colorless
face. "And in exceptionally fine looks, I might add."

"Thank you," Ann replied distantly. "Coffee, Mr.
Briggs?" She put out her hand to ring for the footman.

"Oh, that would be ever so pleasant," Mr. Briggs
replied in his high-pitched voice, gazing at her as if he
had been struck from behind with a blunt instrument.

He might, Ann reflected, be a genius at business,
but she had always found Mr. Briggs singularly lacking in both personality and sensibility. Her father's
awkward attempts at throwing her together with the
junior London manager never failed to irritate her.
Couldn't he see that she wasn't interested in a man
without a chin or a sense of humor? Especially when
that man reminded her of nothing so much as the
mummies in the British Museum. In fact, she was
almost certain that those long dead Egyptians were
more exciting than Mr. Briggs, with his voice like
rustling paper.

"Miss Ann, I hope you will allow me the opportunity of escorting you to a concert of ancient music at
the Anthenum on Tuesday next, I understand that the
great Biloxi is to play the celeste, and I know how
fond you are of music—"

In a moment, Ann knew, Mr. Briggs's hand would
steal out and cover her own on the tabletop. Just as

she was about to prudently drop her hand into her lap, Addle appeared with a discreet cough and laid the coffee tray before her.

She was thus able to occupy herself with the silver pot and the Staffordshire cups, while Addle and a footman hovered nearby, discreetly removing the covers. Private conversation before the servants was, of course, impossible.

Mr. Ingersoll cleared his throat and rattled his papers. "I say, Jeremy, it's about those twenty hogsheads of *vin ordinaire* from Ste. Eliphas—"

Mr. Briggs rose and moved toward his employer, enabling Ann to escape, with only a grateful look at Addle.

"Louisa has her problems," she thought as she hurried up the stairs to the sanctuary of her room, "and I have mine!"

"Of course, you do realize that this may present certain problems for us," Johannes said to the shadowy figure.

Night had long since fallen on the city, and the revellers were all home and hopefully in their own beds, sleeping off the excesses of the departure celebrations for Prince Theo and his delegation, who started their journey to London on the morrow. A cool wind stirred the bits of confetti and castoff flowers around their feet. Above their heads, the ancient statue of Alois the Defender (1289–1341) brooded, his marble stare eternally frozen on the open courtyards of the palace.

But Johannes and his companion had chosen the sinister shadows beneath his feet in which to meet, sheltered from prying eyes and ears by the stone cloister.

"All you need do is play your part. The rest will be taken care of by another member of the prince's entourage. Then when Theo is out of the way, I shall be Crown Prince of Batavia," Johannes said thoughtfully.

His companion nodded. "There can be no suspicion. It will happen abroad. Your ascension to the throne will be immediate, Your Highness."

Johannes drew his cloak closer about himself, looking around into the shadows. "There must be no mistake," he said. "It's my neck not yours, if this fails."

"Oh, yes. It cannot fail, Your Highness. We have planned it for many months. There will be no mistake."

Johannes smiled grimly. "Very well, then." he said.

"When we meet again, I shall have the honor of serving Your Highness, Crown Prince Johannes of Batavia."

The shadow was gone as swiftly as it had come, vanishing back into the darkness, with not even a footfall to mark its exit.

Johannes smiled, making his way back to his quarters with a light step and a tune on his lips.

Vanity had always been his fatal flaw.

3

"*It would seem that* all of London has come out to see the lion," Colonel Rodney murmured to Prince Theodoric as they surveyed the crowded rooms.

"The lion?" Prince Theo asked, running an uncomfortable finger around the high stock of his full-dress uniform. He felt as if he were weighted down by all the badges, ribbons, medals, and orders that his valet, Murdo, had pinned to his uniform for this evening's grand reception at the Batavian Embassy.

"You are the lion," Colonel Rodney explained, "and everyone has come to see you." He was highly amused. But then, Theo reflected, he could afford to be. No protocol forced Colonel Rodney to stand on his feet for hours on end, in the middle of a dull reception line, shaking hands with so many people that his fingers throbbed. His jaw ached too, from the professional smile he had maintained for what seemed to him to be forever, and his feet, crunched into gleaming dress boots, yearned for release.

The cream of London and diplomatic society had turned out for this event, and the state rooms of the embassy were filled as deep as they could hold with people in their most glittering and formal attire.

"I *feel* like a lion. I have never been stared at so much in my life." Colonel Rodney took two glasses of Batavian champagne from a passing waiter, handing one to the prince. "I was beginning to wonder if I had something on my nose," Theo added ruefully.

"Better get used to it. You are the cynosure of all eyes. And why not? A hero, a reigning prince, and a handsome, eligible bachelor who is rumored to be looking for a suitable wife must needs be the focus of the Season." The colonel took a sip of his champagne. "In fact, I could point out to you all the marriage-minded ladies, all the matchmaking mamas, all the toadeaters, the Captain Sharps, and the legs in attendance tonight."

"It is nothing like it was when we were at University," Theo said ruefully. "Then, no one was interested in a foreign student."

"You were not a reigning prince in those days, but a scrubby undergraduate with dubious prospects in a country overrun by Bonaparte. Isn't it interesting how things can change?"

"Very." Theo took another sip of his champagne. "Here comes Baroness Hertzwig. Our ambassadress has that look in her eye that means I must meet yet some more Important People."

A large, self-possessed female with a great many

tall feathers in her turban was making her away across the floor toward them with what appeared to be two young ladies in her wake.

"Hark! More Important People dead ahead!" Colonel Rodney said mischievously. "That's my cousin Louisa Coldstone!"

"We seem to have been ambushed, Rodney. Undone!" The prince muttered beneath his breath.

"Not at all, Highness. I see an escape route if we pretend we do not see them and make our way toward the card room. Our pretext shall be making the acquaintance of one or another of the Carleton House Set, who we may be sure to find there. Get a word in with the Regent, don't you know."

"He who fights and runs away lives to fight another day," the prince replied, and the two young men turned with every appearance of casual nonchalance, strolling in the direction of the card room. "Lead the way, Colonel, we're in your territory now."

"Fear not, Highness, your faithful native guide will show you the escape route perfected by many happy years of bachelorhood."

With only the smallest twinge of guilt, the prince allowed his friend to lead him down a narrow hallway, through the conservatory, and out onto a terrace that looked out over the Embassy garden.

From the basements, the sound of the servants laboring to produce tray after tray of crab patties and champagne echoed through the urban canyons. The distant tinkle of champagne glasses and the low murmur of voices gave a contrapuntal harmony to the equally distant sound of the string quartet in the Reception Room.

The Batavian Embassy was small, but, the prince was gratified to find, popular.

"Remind me to give Hertzwig a medal. Actually, it should go to Madam Hertzwig, since she seems to be the social light," the prince said, withdrawing his cigarillo case from his tunic, offering one to the colonel before striking his firewheel. "They seem to have established diplomatic relations with half the world here."

"Batavian champagne is the attraction," the colonel said, his head wreathed in a cloud of smoke. "People covet invitations to the embassy just to sample the wines, the baron tells me."

"Good for the country," Theo said approvingly. "It's a good endorsement for Batavian—"

He broke off abruptly as the French windows at the other end of the terrace opened and closed quietly and a young woman in a jonquil satin gown emerged, lost in the shadows. Unaware of their presence on the terrace, she seemed to be somewhat agitated, smoothing her gloves and skirt with trembling hands.

In a moment, a burly masculine figure emerged from the doorway, moving toward her. "There you are, my pretty one! Why do you flit away from me when you know that you want this as much as I do—"

The woman, although in shadow, was seen to draw herself up to her full height. "Sir, you presume too much!" she exclaimed in icy tones. "Spare your efforts for someone who would appreciate them!"

Her words must have fallen on deaf ears, for the man seized her, drawing her toward himself.

"Sir, you forget yourself—" she exclaimed angrily.

"No, it's you who forget who I am!" The large man lurched toward her and she stepped back. As the light from the hall fell across the man's face, his eye-patch became visible. But the features of His Royal Highness, the Duke of Cumberland, brother of the Regent and son of mad King George, were clearly discernible. Dissipation was writ large on his swollen, purple countenance. His sinister reputation hung about him in an almost palpable aura.

Colonel Rodney hesitated; for him it was a delicate question of *lesse majeste*. But the Crown Prince of Batavia did not falter. The sight of a damsel in possible distress was sufficient to move Theo to action; he cast down his cigarillo and approached the pair. "May I be of some assistance?" he asked coolly. "Your Royal Highness?"

"Here now, this isn't any of your affair—" the Duke of Cumberland growled, then broke off as the light fell across the prince's face. "Your Highness," he added, lamely. Outranked, outflanked, and outgunned, the baneful old solider fell into retreat.

Mumbling an excuse, Cumberland fell away from the young lady. "Doesn't matter anyway," he said sourly. "She stinks of the shop, if you ask me!"

"The lady has made it clear that your attentions are unwelcome," the Batavian prince replied. Swiftly, his hand shot out, spinning the Royal Duke about by his shoulder so that he staggered. Clearly, he had drunk too much, for it took him several moments to regain an unsteady balance.

"How dare you handle a Royal Duke?" the man exclaimed, when he had disengaged himself from the potted palm he had fallen into.

"Careful!" Randolph said, sauntering over. "You don't want to make him call you out, sir! Prince Theodoric is one of the best shots in Europe!"

The duke's face took on an interesting cast. He backed away, hands up in a defensive position. Rings flashed on his thick fingers. "All apologies, Your Highness! I had no idea it was you—forgive me!"

"You are not welcome here, sir! Begone at once!" Prince Theodoric said coldly.

"I say, you can't talk to *me* in that fashion!" Cumberland fumed, gasping with indignation. "I am a Royal Duke!" he reiterated.

"And this is the Embassy of Batavia, and as such is Batavian soil," Prince Theodoric replied. "I bid you good night sir!"

Thwarted, Cumberland turned, but at the doorway, he looked back at Theo. "I won't forget this, sir!" he growled.

"See that you do not!" Theo replied.

With that, the Duke shot him a baleful look and disappeared.

"You really must drop a hint in Baroness Hertzwig's ear about inviting Prinny and his brothers. Not the done thing, you know!" Colonel Rodney murmured. "Especially Cumberland! A nasty job he is. Supposed to have murdered his first wife, you know."

After watching to be certain he was gone, Theo

turned his attention toward the woman. "Are you all right, ma'm?" he asked. "May I be of some assistance to you?"

She looked up at him, surprised, and drew into the pool of light from the interior of the house, so that he could see that she was a young woman a little above the medium height, with dark hair and a pair of gray eyes, which at this moment were snapping with anger.

"Be of assistance?" she repeated, nervously twisting the tassel of her fan through her fingers. Her tone was not at all that of a lady in distress, but that of one who was greatly annoyed. "I do not need your assistance, sir! I was perfectly capable of depressing that odious man's pretensions without any help from you or anyone else!"

"I merely sought to help you—" Theo stammered, taken aback by this unexpected response.

"Just like a man, to assume that all females are weak and helpless," she snapped, greatly aggrieved. "You could help me if you know a way to remove me from this place! How I despise these gatherings, and these people! Can you imagine being dragged here, all for some dubious European prince?"

That "dubious European prince" was rendered nonplused. His companion, however, was not.

"Ann?" Colonel Rodney exclaimed. "Ann Ingersoll, is that you?"

She looked past Theo, then gasped. "Randolph! Can that be *you*? Oh, thank God, someone who is a familiar face! How did you get trapped into this deadly gathering?"

Colonel Rodney advanced toward her, his hands outstretched, a mischievous smile playing across his features. "Dearest Ann, I find you looking very charmingly. To answer your question—" he bowed and kissed her hand "—I am here because my friend, Prince Theodoric von Hazloe und Gottfreund is here. Your Highness, may I present my old friend, Miss Ann Ingersoll?"

Prince Theodoric and Miss Ingersoll regarded each other. Warily, the prince extended his hand.

"I *am* sorry, Your Highness," Miss Ingersoll said as she offered him her own. He was amazed at the firmness of her grip. "I meant no aspersions upon *you!*"

"I should hope not," he said coolly. He was not used to being rebuffed and insulted by females he had just rescued. "In my country, young ladies are generally well chaperoned enough to prevent this sort of unpleasantness."

"And in *my* country, Prince Theodoric, guests ordinarily don't include persons who force their unwanted attentions on others!"

"Mate and checkmate," Colonel Rodney chuckled. "Here now, the pair of you!" He cleared his throat. "Miss Ingersoll and my cousin Lady Louisa Coldstone have been bosom bows since their school days."

This news did little to lift the prince's sense of ill-use. He seriously questioned the sort of education that would allow anyone to be so discourteous.

For her part, Ann regarded the prince curiously. So, she thought, this was the man who meant to pay court to Louisa! She felt a stab of pity for her friend. He was certainly not a grotesque in looks, she admitted grudgingly, but she sensed that he was one of those sporting, soldierly types who thought all women were fragile, helpless creatures either too stupid or too weak to help themselves.

The prince's evaluation of Miss Ingersoll was no more prepossessing. She was not unattractive, he decided, but too dark to be his type. And her manners, well, they left a great deal to be desired! Aware that most people treated him with the deference due his rank, he was nonetheless a little startled and perhaps even offended by her lack of grace. After all, he had only been trying to help a lady. The old adage, *no good deed goes unpunished* came to his mind.

"I do not recall Englishwomen being quite so—forceful," he said.

Ann bit her lip. She knew she had been churlish, but it was not every day that she found herself pursued by decadent old rogues, or rescued from awkward situations by young and arrogant princes.

"Perhaps we ought to return to the reception," Colonel Rodney suggested tactfully.

"Yes, I think that would be advisable," Theo agreed, smoothing out his gloves. He turned on his heel, frowning. What a rude girl! he thought.

Randolph offered her his arm. "I must say, Ann, you are looking very becomingly tonight in spite of all," he said. "I am sorry about that ugly scene, my dear," he added in an undertone.

Ann shook her head and smiled weakly. "It would seem that *some* persons of rank think because my father is in trade that I am some kind of—of—a doxy!" she confided in a low tone. "I should never have come to this, but Louisa insisted, and Papa seconded her. You know how it is! They think that I should go out more often!"

"I have not seen my cousin tonight. How does she go on?" Randolph asked.

"Most anxious to meet the prince," Ann said dryly. "You seem to have laid the ground well, Randolph!"

He patted her hand. "Trust me, he really is a fine fellow. You shouldn't depress his pretensions, Ann! Not every girl gets rescued from the Royal Ogre by a royal prince!"

"I have long since given up on fairy tales," Ann replied. "I am a serious woman, you know! Since we last met, my feminist principles have increased, rather than diminished!"

The colonel's lips twitched. "Exactly so!" he contented himself with saying. "But you must admit that Louisa will find the prince fascinating!"

"That is for her to say, not me," Ann replied. "He is not an unhandsome man, however," she added generously. "Oh, Lord, Randolph! Why ever did I come tonight? I've been pursued by a decadent duke and now I've set up the back of Louisa's would-be suitor! D'you think I should have headaches and make you take me home to Berkeley Square?"

"No evening is complete until one has been snubbed by a patroness of Almack's," Randolph replied.

"There is that yet to be endured," Ann said gloomily. "The jumped-up tradesman's daughter endures another snub! The thing of it is, I don't even want to go to Almack's, so that doesn't bother me!"

"Well, they can snub us both at once and save themselves the trouble. I would never be asked to darken their doors, believe me!"

Ann laughed, recovering herself. "In general, you know, I don't mind, but sometimes, it does become wearisome."

"Believe me, Ann, you are no mushrooming toad-eater," Randolph said seriously. "You have nothing to be ashamed of in your manners or your origins."

"And just because you are a younger son without a title or a huge fortune doesn't mean you're an ineligible suitor," she sighed.

"Touché!" Randolph laughed. The foundation of their friendship was based on their mutual feeling that they were outcast from the world in which they moved. It gave them strength to commiserate.

It was on the tip of her unruly tongue to tell him about Louisa's feelings for him, but Ann decided she had gotten herself into enough trouble for one night. "My wretched, wretched habits!" she castigated herself aloud. "Why can I not *think* before I *speak*?"

"Because then you would be someone else, and not the Ann we all know and love!" Randolph laughed. "Here now, my girl. That's enough of that. Come along and have a glass of champagne and hold your head high."

"Oh, I am glad that you have come back! It seemed as if you were abroad forever! What did you find to occupy your time in Europe all those months?"

"Business for Whitehall, of a diplomatic and secret nature, not for inquisitive girls barely out of the schoolroom," Randolph replied lightly. "I must, you know, earn my bread. A half-pay, peacetime, sold-up officer must needs earn his bread by the sweat of his brow. A younger son, you know, has two choices; the military or the clergy. I chose the first because no one, not even you, could ever picture a great rogue like me in the pulpit."

Ann laughed. The colonel's humor often restored her own. "I am sorry I offended your royal friend," she admitted.

"Oh, he's not such a bad fellow once you get to know him," the colonel promised her. "Like all royals, he's a bit high in the instep, but he was a ferocious hero in the war. Went through all sorts of hardships and hell-for-leather against the French. Look, ain't that my relation Her Grace over there? Is Louisa with her? Good. Watch and learn, Ann. This is how it is all done."

Baroness Hertzwig, her tall plumes nodding, moved majestically across the floor toward them. She was not to be deprived of her lion, her expression said. While she was far too well bred to betray her annoyance with her sovereign for disappearing, the way in which she bowed to him made Theo feel like a naughty schoolboy. "If Your Highness pleases," she said in ice water tones, "there are a number of distinguished persons present who wish to be presented to you."

"Forgive me, dear baroness!" Theo pleaded earnestly. "I am completely at your disposal!"

The baroness's plumes quivered, but she merely kicked her train out of the way as she looped her arm through the prince's elbow and nodded in the direction of the Duchess of Coldstone.

"Your Highness, may I present the Duchess of Coldstone and her daughter, Lady Louisa Coldstone?" she asked, almost quivering with triumph in this, her greatest social moment.

To say that Prince Theo and Lady Louisa sized each up would have been unspeakably vulgar, but to Ann, witnessing this meeting, it was all too apparent that that was exactly what was happening.

For Louisa's sake, she hoped for Love At First Sight, for fireworks and music that only the prince and Lady Louisa could hear. Alas, it was not be so.

The duchess, resplendent in the famous Coldstone emeralds, dropped a curtsey; Lady Louisa, in the virginal pink pastels suitable to a debutante, followed her mother's lead.

Prince Theo's manners were perfect; he bowed gracefully over the duchess's hand, he nodded toward Lady Louisa, who nodded back.

If there was any instant attraction there, it must have been so subtle that both parties missed it entirely; neither one as much as smiled at the other.

"I am very honored to meet you," Prince Theo said, very correctly, to the duchess.

"And my daughter and I are honored to meet Your Highness," she replied punctiliously.

"I hope I shall be allowed to call upon you while I am in London," the prince said to the duchess.

"We shall look forward to receiving you." The duchess nodded graciously.

"Your Grace, Lady Louisa." The prince nodded.

Both ladies inclined their heads and the baroness, responding to some internal signal born of years of practice on the social circuit, led them away. But not before Louisa shot a speaking look at Randolph. It was an infinitesimal gesture that lasted a second, but Ann saw it. Even Lady Lousia's rigid training could not overcome her emotions in that tiny moment.

For his part, the prince sighed an almost inaudible sigh and followed the ladies across the room with the air of a man wishing himself one thousand miles away.

But Colonel Randolph Rodney did not seem to see it; he was preoccupied with a speck of lint on the lapel of his coat. Was it Ann's imagination or did he seem just a trifle discomfited? Was it possible, she wondered, that the unlucky colonel might have tender feelings for his unattainable cousin? If so, why was he throwing her at the head of this foreign prince?

Before she could consider this point any further, she was aware that a strange man was standing beside her, smiling in a most charming manner. He was the very picture of fashion in the diplomatic corps. A red sash and several miniature decorations adorned the front of his black evening coat. His dark hair was brushed *a la brute*. There was something spoiled and handsome in his countenance that was wickedly attractive. Almost, Ann thought, diabolically tempting. But then, the devil should be handsome and tempting, she reflected. She had just not expected him to have such a charming smile.

"I say, Colonel Rodney, will you introduce me?" he asked.

Randolph shot the man a look of disguised hostility.

"Of course," he responded tonelessly, "Count Johannes von Hazloe, may I present Miss Ingersoll?"

Johannes's smile grew even broader. He took Ann's hand, sweeping a low bow over it. "I am enchanted, Mademoiselle Ingersoll," he said, looking up at her as if to gauge his effect. He held her hand just a little longer than necessary.

"And I am charmed," Ann replied honestly.

"Count von Hazloe is Prince Theodoric's cousin," Randolph said helpfully, if without any noticeable enthusiasm.

"I am attached to the prince's mission," Johannes remarked brightly. "This is my first trip to England, you see." His English, slightly more accented than the prince's, had a lilt that gave his speech a slight questioning rise at the end of each sentence.

"Are you enjoying your stay?" Ann asked a little breathlessly.

"I am now," Johannes replied, gazing into Ann's eyes.

Colonel Rodney cleared his throat.

"Miss Ingersoll was complaining about a headache. I was about to escort her home," he said repressively.

"*Tant pis!*" Johannes sighed.

"I am feeling much more the thing now," Ann said.

"Ah, but I know your headaches," the colonel said. "They are likely to strike at any time."

Johannes cast an amused look at the colonel. "Perhaps we will meet again when you are less, ah, *déprimé.* I sincerely hope so."

"As do I," Ann replied.

"So, it is not good-bye, *mais adieu*," the count sighed.

Randolph all but swept Ann out of the room.

"What in the world?" she asked. "We haven't even thanked our hostess!"

"Send her a note in the morning!" Randolph replied curtly. "Go get your wrap from the cloakroom."

"What about the duchess? I came with Louisa, you know!" Ann exclaimed. "Randolph, what is this all about?"

"Explain to you in the carriage! Explain to my cousin on the way out. I'll meet you in the foyer."

Ann decided that one scene was quite enough for the evening.

Although she was burning with curiosity, she made her way to the cloakroom and fetched her cloak.

As she was standing in the marble foyer, waiting for Randolph to make her excuses, she caught a glimpse of Louisa and the prince, seated on a sofa. Perhaps it was the presence of the Duchess of Coldstone on the prince's other side, very much the chaperone, but it appeared as if they were having trouble finding conversation within the rigid bounds of formal etiquette.

Ann's heart went out to her friend. She knew that the courtship that commenced tonight was a mere formality; whether or not Louisa and her prince found common ground, they were still bound to marry; it was what was expected of them from birth.

And it made her more than ever determined that nothing like that should ever happen to her. Not, of

course, that she would ever be expected to marry a
prince, but—

"Ah, we meet again. I am so sorry about your
headache, Miss Ingersoll," drawled the count, who
seemed to have appeared out of thin air at her side.
He followed her gaze into the crowded salon.
Without hesitation, he picked out the source. "So,
that is the Lady Louisa? *C'est tres belle, ne c'est-ce
pas?*" Johannes had always found that his flirtations
went better if a smattering of French was thrown in.

"She is indeed a great beauty," Ann said. "And a
very dear friend of mine," she added as a subtle
warning.

"Then she is a most fortunate young lady,"
Johannes said. He locked his hands behind his back,
lowering his head as he watched his cousin's public
courtship. A faint smile played around his lips, and
made him look very much like Theo.

In spite of herself, Ann smiled. "I think you are trying to flatter me, Count."

"I only speak what is the truth. Tell me, Miss
Ingersoll, would it be possible to—"

"Ann! Ready to go?"

Randolph's voice, tinged with ill-concealed annoyance, cut through their conversation like a knife.

"Ah, yes," Ann said uncertainly.

Johannes bowed and smiled.

Ignoring him, Randolph bundled Ann into the
night.

"What in the world was that all about?" Ann
demanded as soon as they were in the carriage.

"Count von Hazloe is a dangerous man. He is not

the sort of person that I would wish any friend of mine to know," Randolph said. He withdrew into a corner of the cab, his face hidden in shadow.

"I rather liked him," Ann replied. "I think that I have been out in the world long enough to decide for myself if I like someone or not. He's madly charming."

"Mad perhaps. You know that he is next in line for the throne if anything should happen to Theo—to the prince. The only reason he's with the mission is that the prince likes to have him where he can be watched."

Enlightenment was beginning to dawn upon Ann. She turned and looked wonderingly at Randolph's shadowy profile. "Why, I believe that this didn't have the first thing to do with me! What a bambury tale you told, Randolph! You needed an excuse to leave and I was convenient!"

He said nothing.

Undeterred, Ann pressed on, her unruly tongue running away with her again.

"You're in love with Louisa, aren't you? And you couldn't bear to see her with the Prince of Batavia! I was just an excuse to allow you to leave!" Amazed, she sank back into the cushions.

"Don't be a fool, Ann," the colonel sighed. "Why would she even want to think about me?"

"But she does," Ann burst out before she could check herself. "Louisa's been in love with you forever and ever! She thinks you don't care about her."

Randolph turned toward her so that he faced the light falling from the carriage windows. There was torment in his eyes.

"You have made me at once the happiest and the most miserable man in London," he said slowly. "I hope that this conversation will go no further."

"No—no! Of course not," Ann promised hastily.

"You are intelligent enough to comprehend that there could never be a way for—that I could encourage Louisa! My prospects are dim, at best! Louisa is a Coldstone, and no one knows better than I what that means. From birth, she has been groomed to do her duty by the family. And that means the best marriage she can make. Louisa may look as high as she pleases, and why not? She is the daughter of a duke, from an old and respected family, on which I am just a sprig on a cadet branch! She is beautiful, she is accomplished, she has a large fortune! While I, well, we both know my circumstances. Besides," he added gloomily, "she is young yet. No doubt, if she thinks of me, it's a girlish fantasy."

"Louisa is not the type of female who has girlish fantasies," Ann said firmly. "You should know that."

But Randolph was occupied with his own thoughts. "When I came back from the war, that gawky schoolgirl had turned into a beautiful woman. I knew at once that—but what does it matter?"

"If you love Louisa, why did you introduce her to the Prince of Batavia?" Ann asked.

"People like Louisa and Prince Theodoric do not marry for love. You should know that." Randolph sighed. He crossed his arms over his chest. "Because if she must marry wealth and power, I can think of no man more suitable!" the colonel declared. "Remember, the prince and I were in the wars together. What we went through would have weeded out any weak or dishonorable man. I know that Theo will always treat her as she should be treated, with the utmost consideration. If I cannot marry her, she should have a man of rank who will respect her, and treat her with the consideration she deserves. She was bred to become a princess. It is the best thing."

"Very noble," Ann said. "But what about her feelings? Your feelings?"

"Feelings do not enter into it. When you reach the altitude that the Dukes of Coldstone live upon, the word 'love' is considered vulgar. Louisa knows that as well as I do. Believe me, this is the best way."

Ann shook her head. "I wish," she said quietly. "that I could feel as you do about the Prince of Batavia. But, royalty or not, his manners are certainly not civil."

"You don't know him."

"Nor do I want to. No, I am exhausted by all these fine people! No more royalty for me, plain Miss Ann Ingersoll of Berkeley Square, I beg of you!"

4

"The difficult part about having principles is trying to put them into action when one has no outlet. I cannot write, so that is no good; I cannot teach, so that avenue is closed; I belong to no salon of intellectuals, so that is out. And one hates going about prosing on and on to people who don't have the faintest idea what one is discussing!"

A week or so later found Ann and Louisa together again in the Morning Room at Coldstone House. They were crocheting infant gowns for The London Relief Society, one of the duchess's charities. Although neither of them was a particularly good needlewoman, that aspect of their education being sadly neglected by the excellent Miss Ridgely, Her Grace knew that they could be trusted with the few simple stitches and patterns that went into the manufacture of these simple sacks.

"I just think that we lead useless lives, that's all,"

Ann was saying, her fingers working through the thin, fine wool strands. "It is an excellent thing to have high feminist principles, but it is quite another thing for you and me to put them into practice. We might as well not signify at all. We could be in the seraglio for all we've put our education into practice in this world! Of course, Good Works are important, very important, but there wouldn't be such a need for Good Works if women achieved more rights and opportunities! Instead, what we do is lead lives under our parents' thumbs. And when you marry, you will be the chattel of your husband! At least if we were poor, we would be able to be governesses or educationists! Instead, we lead lives of empty frivolity, supported by our parents!"

"Is that so?" Louisa asked absently. She silently counted out a row of stitches, her fair head bent over her needlework. As much as she loved her friend, there were times when she was simply content to drift away on her own thoughts; Ann's were too convoluted, too passionate for her to follow.

Sensing this, Ann stopped herself in mid-tirade, laughing. "Listen to me run on! Do you remember when we thought we might run away and live in a cottage in Wales, dwindling down into two old spinsters with our books and cats rather than marry?"

"We were young and foolish," Louisa replied evenly. "At least I was." Suddenly, she looked up again. The faint blue blemish beneath her eyes stood out against her alabaster skin, and there was a wary look in her eyes that Ann could not like. One perfect tear formed and rolled down her creamy cheek.

"Oh, what a fool I am!" she exclaimed, casting aside her crochet work. "I ought to be the happiest female in London!" She rose and walked across the room, momentarily agitated out of her usual glacial calm. "Every eligible female—and quite a few ineligible females—are swooning over him!"

Ann rose and followed her friend. She put her arm around Louisa's shoulders. "Dearest Louisa! Whatever is the matter?" she asked, although she was certain she knew.

Louisa put her fair head on Ann's shoulder. "I'm all right now, really I am," she said in a voice that was only a little shaken. She looked at Ann and smiled a thin, wintry smile. "It's all just a little overwhelming. Everything is happening, and it seems as if I have no say in my own future."

"It's the prince, isn't it?" Ann's disapproval was strong in her voice.

"Oh, it's not Prince Theodoric!" Louisa said quickly. "His understanding is quite superior, and his manners everything that is civil! Well, he *seems* that way, anyway," she added dubiously. "We're hardly ever alone, you know. Mama or someone is always present. He dances very well, however! Last night at Almack's, we waltzed. It's all so awkward! We both know that we're supposed to become engaged, and we barely know what to say to each other!"

"I didn't find him all that grand," Ann said. "In fact, I found him rather high in the instep."

"Well, he is a prince," Louisa said. "And Mama says that it would be a very good thing for me to be a princess."

"Good for the family, you mean. Oh, Louisa, if you don't want to marry him, don't! Didn't you learn *anything* from Miss Ridgely?"

"Miss Ridgely isn't a Coldstone," Louisa replied.

For that, Ann had no answer. Her conversation with Colonel Rodney haunted her, yet she had promised him that she would hold her tongue. While her sense told her that this was the correct course, her sensibility told her otherwise. Not a romantic by nature, Miss Ingersoll was, nonetheless, a female who liked to see justice done and nature in harmony, and it seemed to her both foolish and tragic that Randolph Rodney and Louisa Coldstone should never be able to make a match of it.

But, if Louisa knew that her feelings for Randolph were reciprocated, Ann reasoned, perhaps—But there was no "perhaps" in the world Louisa occupied. Knowing that Randolph cared for her would only make it that much harder to do her duty. Illogically, this impasse made Ann resent Prince Theodoric. If only he had stayed in Batavia where he belonged, she thought meanly, none of this would have happened.

"Oh, look," Louisa said, pointing out the window.

Ann followed her friend's gaze down to the street, where Prince Theodoric's curricle was pulling up before the house.

"Is it really four o'clock?" Louisa asked, glancing at the clock on the mantelpiece. "No, it's only two, and Mama is still out! What can he mean coming here at this hour, and unannounced? Ann, you must stay with me! I can't see him alone!"

"I'd *like* to see him alone, in a locked room," Ann muttered. Aloud she said, "Of course, Louisa."

As he handed the reins of his borrowed curricle to the bowing footman, Prince Theodoric looked up at the imposing facade of Coldstone House, swallowing hard. Although he knew he was not expected until four, he was hoping against hope that he would catch Lady Louisa at home, for once without attendant mother or chaperone.

For the past week, he had been punctilious in the observation of every convention surrounding a formal courtship. He and Louisa had met in public, under the watchful eye of her parents and a hundred other interested parties. He had dined with her at Lady Jersey's; attended a balloon ascension with her, the duchess, and Princess Lieven; attended the theater with her, her aunt, Lady Dempster, and her uncle, General Hardcastle; and played silver loo with her at the Duchess of Avon's. Last night, he had waltzed with her at Almack's. So far, he had found her to be a well-mannered beauty and little more. If there was any trace of a personality behind that cool, lovely exterior, he had yet to discover it. With both of them acutely aware that they were the object of interest to all London, their conversations had never risen above the commonplace. He knew as little now about her likes and dislikes as he had the first night he met her. Nor did she seem to exhibit any curiosity about him.

Having escaped early from an extremely dull meeting, he had impulsively driven around to Upper Mount Street hoping to catch a moment's private conversation with Lady Louisa. If they were to become betrothed, as everyone seemed to expect, it seemed to him that it was necessary for them to get to know one another. The prince did not hope for a grand passion, but he could hope for understanding, and perhaps, friendship that would deepen into something richer.

With these things in mind, Theo bounded up the steps and rapped smartly on the knocker. He hoped that he was looking his best, in biscuit-colored pantaloons, a pearl-striped waistcoat, and a jacket of brown Bath superfine. Murdo, his valet, had turned him out with a cravat tied in a trone d'amour, and he had every reason to think that he looked fashionable, if not dandyish.

For a man who normally cared little about his dress, Theo had taken pains.

He was admitted to Coldstone House by the butler, whose lofty demeanor concealed a romantic turn of mind. "I think you will find that Lady Louisa is at home in the Morning Room, sir," he informed the prince, all but smiling as he escorted Theo up the grand stairs, a very odd looking cupid indeed. "His Grace is at his club at this hour of the day, and Her Grace is generally visiting her sister."

Lady Louisa looked very pretty in a simple round gown of pale blue kerseymere that matched her eyes. When the butler announced the prince, she looked up and then rose, dropping a pretty curtsey.

The butler, beaming, closed the doors behind him, going downstairs to loftily inform the footman that His Highness was about to come up to scratch or he didn't know nothing.

The prince smiled and bowed, presenting her with a nosegay of white tea roses. At last, he thought. Then, with a sinking heart, he saw that they were not alone.

All of Theo's hopes for a serious tête-à-tête were dashed when he saw Miss Ingersoll seated at the table in the center of the room.

"Ah, Your Highness," she said brightly, a faint, mocking smile playing about her lips.

"Your Highness, you know Miss Ingersoll," Lady Louisa said, bidding him be seated. "As you can see, we are engaged in making infant's gowns for the London Relief Society, one of my mother's charities."

"Yes, we crochet and crochet," Ann said, holding up a shapeless mass for his inspection.

Theo would have liked to say that he pitied any infant that had to be dressed in such a formless garment, but he restrained himself, smiling his most mocking smile. "Very commendable," he said tonelessly.

Ann might have read his thoughts, for she smiled in return, a bright, glittering smirk that showed she knew exactly what he thought about her and that *her* thoughts about *him* were twice as unflattering.

Lady Louisa sat down and resumed her crocheting. There was a long and not very comfortable silence.

During the silence, Theo cast a meaningful look at Ann, who smiled, seemingly oblivious to his message.

"So what brings you to Grosvenor Square, sir?" Ann asked him at last.

"A conference that ended early. I had a moment

and I thought that I might be able to persuade Lady Louisa, if she had no other plans, to take a drive in the park with me," Theo said.

"Thank you very much, perhaps another day," Louisa replied. "As you can see, I have Miss Ingersoll here."

"Besides, everyone knows the fashionable hour for the park is five," Ann put in brightly. Wielding a pair of tiny silver scissors, she clipped a bit of yarn with a sharp snip. "That's when I drive my phaeton."

"*Your* phaeton?" Theo asked, surprised out of his hauteur.

"Oh, yes. I have a phaeton and a set of matched grays," Ann replied.

"A very dashing high perch phaeton," Lady Louisa put in. A particularly tricky turn in her stitches forced her to keep her eyes on her needlework as she spoke.

Theo raised one eyebrow. He leaned back slightly in his chair, regarding Ann from beneath his lashes, a faint, dangerous smile playing about the corners of his lips. "Indeed," he said. "A high perch phaeton is hardly a suitable vehicle for a female!"

Ann, seeing that she had succeeded in baiting him, opened her eyes very wide. "Oh, that is what everyone says, until they see my team! They are bruising, you know. I chose them myself!"

"Chose them yourself," the prince said with a slight curl of his lips. "Indeed. It is a great deal too bad that there is no man who can be trusted to chose your horses for you."

"Oh, my father says I have a much better eye for horseflesh than he does," Ann remarked blithely.

"Females," Prince Theo said through gritted teeth, "tend to be ham-handed in their handling of the ribbons. In my experience. Do you drive, Lady Louisa?"

"In the country, I have my little cabriolet with a mare to draw it," Lady Louisa said. "I don't care much for driving in town. The streets are too crowded, the traffic too intense."

"Ah," the prince said. "And do you ride?"

"Oh, never in town. I don't really like horses, you see," Lady Louisa said.

"Ah," said the prince, who did like horses very much. "What do you like, Lady Louisa?"

He received a startled stare for his pains. "Gardening," Lady Louisa said after a moment's thought. No one had ever asked her what she liked before; it was expected that she would enjoy whatever she was told to enjoy. After all, she was a Coldstone. "I like gardening."

"We have some very fine gardens in my country. My mother was particularly fond of roses," the prince offered.

"Oh, really? What varieties did she grow?" Louisa asked with interest.

Unfortunately, the prince could not remember, if he had ever known at all. "Uh, there were some pink ones and some red ones," he offered, "and white. She was very fond of white ones. I always think that gardens are one of the few areas where female instinct is naturally superior to that of men."

A small strangled sound emerged from Ann's lips. She felt Louisa's small, slippered foot kicking her beneath the table and swallowed hard.

"Ah," Louisa said quickly. "How very interesting. I understand that champagne is the principal export of your country, Your Highness?"

"Ah, yes. We are famous for the quality of our champagne. Do you like champagne, Lady Louisa?"

"It makes me sneeze, unfortunately," she replied.

"Batavia has a particularly salubrious climate for the champagne grape," Ann put in helpfully. "The elevation of the mountains and the quantity of the rainfall are exactly right for producing a fine grape. The climate is particularly suited to noble rot, I believe."

Theo turned to stare at her. For a moment, he allowed himself to be impressed, then his dislike of Ann reasserted itself and his lip curled slightly. "You seem to know a great deal about champagne, Miss Ingersoll. In general, I have found that men are superior judges of wine. Women tend to like anything that is sweet."

"*This* poor female does know a great deal about champagne. You might say it was in the blood," Ann responded sweetly. "And, I might add, I know horses." She was too angry to laugh at his deliberate goading. It was clear to her that he wanted her to find some excuse to leave him alone with Louisa. And it was becoming clear to him that she intended to remain firmly in place.

How dare she? he thought. No one ever gainsaid his wishes! He was a prince!

There was more silence. The tick of the clock and the hiss of coal in the gate marked the passage of time.

Theo looked out the window and wished that he

were at home in Batavia. Ann frowned to herself, selecting her next target. Louisa kept her eyes on her crocheting.

"Such lovely weather for this time of year," the prince said, trying a new tack. "Don't you agree, Lady Louisa?"

"Yes," she said. "We are fortunate. Generally, by this time of year, it is quite chilly."

"This is why England is not favorable for the production of wines. We lack the temperance of climate, the sunlight, and the steady warmth that is so necessary to good vineyard yield."

"One might think that you were a vintner, Miss Ingersoll. You seem to know so much about grapes."

"By that same token, you should be at Tattersall's since you know so much about horses," Ann said sweetly.

"At least I talk about what I know," Theo was stung into replying.

"And you think you know about horses?" Ann asked, eyes narrowing. Ann's expression was taking on a particularly mulish set that Louisa knew and dreaded.

No one had ever challenged Prince Theodoric von Hazloe's authority so directly since he had left the schoolroom many years ago. His princely dignity wounded, he leaned forward. "And what do you know about horses?"

"Enough to know that your left leader is a rum go," Ann replied. "Spavined, I would imagine!"

"Is that so, dear lady? Allow me to correct your— your female misapprehensions!" Theo replied testily.

"I have been choosing my own horses since I was old enough to ride, and no one has ever faulted my judgments!"

"I really don't think—" Louisa put in, horrified at this turn of events.

"Mere cattle," Ann plunged on heedlessly. Why did he annoy her so much? It was almost as if he were trying his best to plague her. "Perhaps you should see my pair!"

"Yes, perhaps I should!" Theo retorted. "You say that you drive at five in the park? We shall meet there and see whose horses are the best!"

"As Your Highness wishes," Ann replied coolly. "Shall we say one day at five-thirty at the West Gate?"

"Done!" Theo agreed.

Louisa looked from one of them to the other, rendered speechless by sheer horror. "Ann, I think this is headed in an extremely improper direction," she warned.

"Nonsense! What could possibly be improper about comparing two teams? You must remember, Louisa, that I do not live under the same strictures that you do! What do you think, that I'll be denied vouchers for Almack's?" Miss Ingersoll laughed.

"Ann!" Louisa cried, much shocked. "Please don't talk like that!"

"I must take my leave now," Theo said quickly. He had decided to chose discretion over valor. Dignity offended, his pride stung, he was keenly aware of an impulse to deliver the impertinent Miss Ingersoll a sharp set down. Only the presence of Lady Louisa prevented him from telling her exactly what an ill-bred piece of baggage she was. "Five-thirty Thursday," he said through gritted teeth, bowing to Louisa and taking his leave.

"Agreed!" Ann called to his back. "Your Highness," she added as an afterthought.

After the doors had closed behind him, Louisa turned to look at Ann with wide eyes. "Whatever are you doing?" she asked.

"Putting that odious man in his place!" Ann smoldered.

"But he's a prince!"

"Be that as it may, he's still an odious, stupid, toplofty man who has done nothing to deserve the high opinion in which he holds himself! It's time someone put him in his place!"

"Oh, dear," Louisa said.

5

While his cousin Theo had been fully occupied in a whirlwind of official banquets, receptions, conferences, and appearances, Johannes had been enjoying himself immensely in London. The British people, still floating on a tide of goodwill since the end of the long wars, welcomed him everywhere he went, and all doors were open to him. His enormous charm, his cynical wit, his good looks and graceful manners were enough to make him well liked among superficial acquaintances. But then, Johannes never sought out more than superficial friendship with any other being, his sincere affection reserved entirely for himself.

Besides, it made it so much simpler for him, knowing that when he left London behind, a brace of cuckolded husbands and a sheaf of unpaid gaming debts would not overly trouble his conscience. As Theo discerned, Johannes was blissfully untroubled by the moral impediments of lesser mortals.

Being of a naturally lethargic disposition, he did not bestir himself overmuch to create any problems for his cousin. His entire energies were given over to his own pleasures. When opportunity struck, he would take advantage of it. But never, ever would he go out of his way . . .

Johannes liked the ladies, as Ann Ingersoll had discovered, and he was pleased that the ladies returned his regard a hundredfold. The pleasant result was a series of assignations where his companions ranged from peeresses to chambermaids. As long as all parties involved understood that no permanent connection was being formed in a single dalliance, this seemed like a harmless enough diversion to him. Although his sense of self-preservation was too finely honed to allow him to dally with young and virginal females, so very dull, so very likely to have angry fathers and brothers, the field was still full of challenges.

Likewise, he was pleased to note that his quasi-royal status gave him entree to every gaming club in the Metropolis from the very highest reaches to the very lowest hells. White's and Watiers' knew him well. He played faro for pound points and deep basset for guinea stakes, and his vowels were accepted when he lost, which, unfortunately, he did with a depressing regularity. No one would dream of pressing a member of the Batavian entourage for immediate payment, and a casual murmur about exchange rates and a mislaid letter of credit was usually enough to reassure his creditors. After all, a gentleman always paid his gaming debts.

Alas, Johannes was not only no gentleman, but planned to be far and away before matters reached a point where someone might actually pressure him to pay his debts.

Small wonder there was no time for him to consider ways and means to eliminate his cousin. "There just aren't enough hours in the day," he sighed to himself as he sipped his morning chocolate, basking in the noonday sun that seeped through his curtains. If his nocturnal habits inconvenienced Baroness Hertzwig's staff, it mattered not to him. He glanced through a stack of invitations that had been placed on his breakfast tray and sighed. The Countess Redmond's costume ball; really, it would be so amusing, he must think of some really clever costume. And . . .

"I really *must* think of some way to dispose of Theo," he said to himself. "But not this very minute," he added, falling back against the pillows to study a very indiscreet note from Lady Redmond, prattling and full of gossip, including the interesting news that Prince Theo and a Miss Ingersoll were said to have engaged to race their vehicles in the park at five-thirty. Was it, Lady Redmond wanted to know, true? Her footman awaited his reply.

"What? What? Theo actually having a frolic?" Johannes asked out loud, unbelieving. He rubbed his eyes and reread her ladyship's crabbed hand again. Johannes mentally castigated himself for not keeping himself better informed of his cousin's activities. He frowned, sighed, excused himself, and wrinkled his brow in thought.

Suddenly, Inspiration struck. Lady Redmond forgotten, Johannes sat up in bed, smiling. "Of course!" he said. "Why didn't I think of that before? How clever I am!"

If Ann had known Johannes's thoughts, she might have considered agreeing with them. "Odious, abominable, overbearing!" were some of the words she had used to describe Theo to her groom as they departed Berkeley Square that afternoon. "He ought to be boiled in oil!"

Joseph Potter, who had mounted Ann on her first pony and taught her how to drive to an inch, wasted no words. "Don't take on, Miss," he admonished. "Keep your mind on them hosses. They're awful fresh to hand."

As they turned smartly out of the mews and proceeded down the street at a handsome pace, Ann had every reason to think that she presented a very nice appearance. She wore a driving dress of dove gray, which matched her eyes, trimmed with yellow silk braid. On her dark hair, she wore a smart felt toque trimmed with a set of dashing scarlet plumes that curled over her cheek. Black jean boots and gloves of york tan completed her ensemble.

Her phaeton, a present from her father upon her graduation from Miss Ridgely's, was a triumph of the carriage maker's trade. A delicate body was slung over yellow wheels at an alarming distance from the ground, the seat was squabbed with tooled leather, and the brasses shone with polish. A high stickler might declare it no proper vehicle for a lady, but no one could say that her horses were not a pair of elegant high steppers.

Fine-boned matched grays, complete to a shade, they moved at a smart trot down the street, responding to Ann's light hand on the ribbons with a restive energy. In spite of Joseph Potter's admonition, she was able to keep them well in hand.

He crossed his arms over his chest, nodding his approval. He had taught her well, and she did him credit, he reflected, although no trace of his pride showed on his stolid, deceptively sour countenance.

"Mind you behave yourself," he added. "If your dad gets wind of any foolishness, you know who he'll blame and it won't be me," he said.

"He won't hear a word of it from me," Ann promised. "So if he hears from anyone, it would have to be you."

"I ain't one to peach," Joseph Potter said thoughtfully. "Still and all, this prince is said to have a handsome turnout."

"Be that as it may," Ann replied.

She took a corner too sharply to suit him and Joseph clucked his tongue. "Slow down, Missy! Better twenty minutes late in this world than twenty years early in the next!"

Ann collected herself and did her best to drive at a more sedate pace as they wound their way through the bustling London traffic in the direction of Hyde Park. Her driving was so circumspect that Joseph nodded approvingly as she overtook a delivery cart and reined within several inches of sparing a collision with a dowdy laudaulet coming the other way.

"Just remember you're a fine whip, but by no means as fine as you think you are and you'll be all right," Joseph advised stolidly. "A good driver knows his limits and never overshoots the mark!"

"Yes, Joseph," Ann said meekly.

Beneath the autumn shade of old elms, Prince Theo, accompanied by Colonel Rodney, was waiting with his curricle and his bays at the West Gate. He was not in the best of moods. "I can't believe that I have agreed to this meeting," he grumbled. "Every time I see this female, she seems to find a way to discomfort me! And I don't like it, Rodney! Not at all!"

Colonel Rodney laughed. "I should have warned you about Ann—Miss Ingersoll, I should say! She has that effect on some people! She says exactly what is on her mind. Of course, she can, for her father is immensely wealthy and—she has embraced women's rights."

"I seem to have noticed some mumblings on the subject. Among other crackbrained notions!" Theo turned the reins in his fingers, and the bays, sensitive to the movement, snorted and stirred restlessly. "I cannot imagine her team would be finer than mine," he said. "I picked these horses out at Tattersall's myself."

"They are fine horses," Colonel Rodney assured him. For his part, he was rather amused by this whole affair. How, he wondered, could two people of whom he was so fond find themselves at such daggers drawn? "But then, so are Miss Ingersoll's grays."

As if on cue, Miss Ingersoll's phaeton swept through the gates. It must be said that Prince Theo's gaze fell upon her, then her horses, with something akin admiration, had he been willing to admit to such a feeling in connection with the detestable female in question, which he was not. He expressed himself by raising his eyebrows. "A fine turnout indeed," he said.

Ann smiled. She was inclined to be gracious. She studied the prince's team with a knowledgeable eye. "Now that I see your team at close inspection, Your Highness, I recall them as being part of old Fortenham's estate! His widow sold them up, I believe! I must say that I approve," she conceded reluctantly. "Nicely formed pair, great goers." She tapped her cheek with her whip and inclined her head. "I wonder how they would go against my grays."

Beside her Joseph, professionally stolid, eyes ahead, arms crossed over his livery, coughed meaningfully.

Ann's eyes danced. She glanced at Theo with just a hint of a droll look. He forgot himself just enough to drop a most unroyal wink. Recovering themselves, they both began to talk in the universal language of equine affectionatos.

"They look like regular out-and-outers to me," the prince said, bending from the curricle seat to give them a visual inspection. "How do they handle?"

"I've taken the freshness out of them on the way to the park, but they're sweet goers nonetheless. You know, I have seen those bays around the Metropolis many times, and I have always yearned to drive them," Ann admitted.

"They may be a little strong for a female to handle," the prince said. But, because he was an honest man, he was forced to admit, "But if you can handle your grays, you may be able to handle my team."

"It takes a special whip to handle my grays," Ann said. "A light hand, a certain . . ."

"Take the reins, Randolph," the prince said, swinging himself down from the curricle.

"Joseph, wait for me here," Ann said.

The groom lowered himself to the pavement with a speaking look at her. "Remember you're never as good as you think you are," he told her in an undertone. "And keep your fingers tight against the leather!"

Prince Theo swung himself easily into the seat the groom had vacated, and Ann handed him the ribbons. "Give them a little head," she said. Her "Oh!" hung in the air.

She clutched her little toque, plumes flying as they took off down the pathway at a gallop, disappearing around a bend.

"You said give them their head!" The prince's voice floated back.

"Rather than leave the horses standing, Joseph, I will wheel them around the Row," the colonel decided, as he watched the phaeton disappear.

"Should I come with you, sir?" the groom asked.

Rodney shook his head. "No, Miss Ingersoll may have need of you before I return. I'll just take them for a round or two," he said, impatient to be moving on. He sawed on the reins and the big bays moved into a brisk walk.

The afternoon was growing a little brisk; the skies were clouding, the great gray billows moving across the London rooftops. A small, sharp breeze had picked up, rustling through the gold and russet leaves. He turned away from the Row and guided the horses down a narrow path along the Serpentine, watching carefully for the presence of another person. But he was fortunate; the pathways were deserted, each curve hidden behind dense foliage. He was alone. He gave the bays their head.

A few minutes later, he guided the horses back toward Rotten Row, the fashionable carriage drive. It would rain before morning, one of the steady gray drizzles for which England was famous. It perfectly matched the colonel's mood. The only event that could possibly enliven his mood, he thought, was a glimpse of Lady Louisa strolling along the paths.

He turned his thoughts toward a vision of that familiar, achingly lovely face, framed by a bonnet trimmed in ribbons of a pink shade known as "heartbreak". . . .

"Randolph," she would say, eyes as blue as the sky. "I did not think to find you here!"

"Hello Louisa," Randolph would say, hoping his voice betrayed none of the aching of his heart. "Come to take the air?"

"No, I've come to plead with you to stop this—this foolishness at once!" she exclaimed. "I cannot live this deception any longer! I love you, Randolph, and I don't care what the world says!"

"Perhaps you ought to allow me to discuss this with you as we take the curricle around the Row," Randolph would suggest.

"Oh, I shouldn't, Mama—" Louisa would say dubiously.

"Come, Cinderella! Your chariot awaits!" Randolph would exclaim as he lifted her up into the curricle. *"I'll take you away from all of this. We'll live in a cottage! We'll subsist on love!*

"We'll . . . "

Louisa would smile shyly at him and . . .

"I say! Colonel! Colonel Rodney! Slow down! *Au succors!"*

Colonel Rodney felt the first breath of coming winter and lifted his face toward the gray heavens. It was then that he saw the familiar figure strolling down the Row toward him. It was as if someone had awakened him from a dream with a clashing noise.

"Johannes!" he ejaculated, surprised, then amused. "On the strut, are you?"

The count waved his handkerchief before his face as he drew abreast of the curricle. "Oh, my dear Rodney, how fortuitous to see you here! I am exhausted! This English *chose*, this walking *pour le sport* is inhuman! It is not civilized! Take me up with you! I am exhausted. My feet hurt! I can't catch my breath!"

The sight of the impeccable Count von Hazloe glowing with perspiration and out of breath from his exertions made Randolph grin in spite of himself. "Oh, very well," he said grudgingly. "Come on, then!"

"A thousand thank yous," Johannes sighed as he

climbed up into the curricle. "Alas, that my cousin does not see fit to provide me with an allowance that would allow me such a vehicle!"

"Your cousin knows you'd bankrupt the treasury if you had your way," Randolph replied.

"I may be expensive, but I am worth it," Johannes replied complacently. He tipped his hat and bowed to a pair of ladies in a passing barouche. They simpered and gestured toward him. "Besides, it is *comme il faut* to be seen at the fashionable hour in the park, and I am *always* a man of style!"

"Yes," Randolph agreed tonelessly.

"But you are driving my cousin's curricle, I see! How does this come about?"

"He is driving with Miss Ingersoll." The press of carriages on the Row was great at that hour, and the colonel was forced to concentrate on his driving. All the world, it seemed, was intent upon taking the air that day. The season was drawing to a close, and the fashionable world was intent upon extracting every pleasure before withdrawing to the country for the winter. As he spoke, Johannes bowed left and right; he lifted his hat; he smiled; he basked in the glow of recognition he received from one and all. In short, he enjoyed his status as lion as much as it was possible for him to enjoy anything. But he seemed to especially enjoy the knowledge that his cousin was driving with a lady.

"With Miss Ingersoll?" he repeated, lifting his eyebrows slightly. "I would think that he would be driving with the very pretty Lady Louisa, would you not?"

"I wouldn't know," Colonel Rodney replied. He did not like to hear her name on the count's lips. It was almost a sullied sound.

"Yes, the charming Miss Ingersoll! Hardly the type of female one would expect our prince to take driving. Ah, there is the soigné Princess Lieven. Good afternoon, Princess. A shame about her skin, isn't it?" he added in an undertone. "She's as yellow as old muslin."

"I wouldn't know. I barely know the woman. What's your game, Johannes?"

The count made such a show of casting his face in an innocent expression that Randolph knew at once that he had been up to something.

"A gallop in the park?" Ann asked, mock-horrified as the prince guided the phaeton around the deserted lane. All of the fashionable world, as they both knew, was taking the air on the more sedate Rotten Row. "Whatever will the ton say?"

"I am the Crown Prince of Batavia," Theo answered quizzically. "What should I care what the ton says?"

"If you aspire to fashion, then you would be better off not to be seen galloping. A canter, a trot, yes. But a gallop, no! It is beyond the pale."

"I see," the prince laughed, and allowed the grays their head. "Then gallop I must!"

They moved at a high pace along the narrow pathways. Once, when they passed through a stone arch, Ann held her breath, but Theo cleared it with inches to spare.

"Very dashing!" Ann said in sincere admiration.

The roadway snaked and turned through dense autumn foliage, sometimes traveling through wooded acres, sometimes easing its way along the Serpentine. Not once did Theo falter on the strange road, although several times Ann thought he might take a curve on two wheels. He smiled, more to himself than for her, happy to be free of the burdens and restraints of office, if only for a short time.

Theo, perhaps feeling after several miles of this that he had proved his point, slowed the team down to a brisk trot. They were traveling along a narrow gravel path through low shrubbery and dense, golden-leafed planes. There was not another soul in sight. The only sound was the brisk strike of the horses' hooves as they hit the gravel. No one walked on the path or drove a carriage along the road. "Not bad," he admitted. "A bit sensitive to the bit, but in general, a pair that I would not disdain to have."

"I'll keep you in mind," Ann said. "I have been thinking about a set of black—"

A sound, a high-pitched whining resonance, sliced through the air. She felt, rather than saw, something pass within a foot of her face, and muffled a cry as Theo startled, then pushed her down into the seat.

"Stay down!" he cried, covering her with his body. The horses, sensing something amiss, whinnied, straining at the traces, and Theo cursed softly in his native language as he used all of his strength to control them from a bolt. They took off, panicked.

"What in the world—" Ann cried, startled out of her composure.

"Stay down!" the prince commanded, up righting himself. He sawed on the reins, pulling them tightly into his body. The phaeton lurched and wobbled precariously on its high yellow wheels, fragile balance shifting from side to side as the frightened horses galloped madly down the pathway.

It took about two minutes for Theo to bring the grays back into control, but for Ann, peering up from the fenders, it seemed like hours. Finally, the horses slowed, exhausted by fright, then grew calmer. Using all of his strength, Theo was finally able to coax them to a skittish walk.

"Are you all right? Hold the reins," he commanded, throwing them to Ann as he jumped down and went to take the horse's heads. He spoke soothingly to them as they tried to drag him along, and Ann held them from bolting again. He was, she noted, very good with them; whatever he said, they seemed to regain their calm. She wished that she could say the same for herself. She was still shaking when he came back and helped her down.

"What was that?" she asked, fluttering out her skirts as soon as her feet were planted firmly on solid ground, "I've never seen them panic like that before—"

Theo had taken the left mare by the bridle and was walking the team back up the path, looking carefully to the right and the left.

"A ball," he said grimly. "From a pistol. I haven't heard that sound in years, but once you hear it, you never forget it."

Ann had to run to catch up with him. She picked up her skirts and looked around, as if expecting someone to emerge from the bushes. "Someone took a shot at us?" she asked, unbelieving. "In the middle of London? In Hyde Park?"

Theo nodded, frowning. "Hold the horses again," he commanded.

She did so, and he strode quickly into the brush, parting the leaves as he went.

"I don't believe this," Ann said uncertainly, keeping the ribbons taut. "Firing guns in the park is strictly forbidden, you know. The park rangers wouldn't like it." City bred, she could not imagine guns being casually discharged in the Metropolis. "Footpads, pickpockets, thieves, yes, but someone with a gun?"

"Here's your proof," Theo said. He returned with his penknife and a small black ball, which he held in his hand for her inspection. "That's from a pistol," he said shortly. "I dug it out of that tree over there. Someone took a shot at us."

"Good Lord!" Ann exclaimed. "D'you suppose someone's playing with a gun here somewhere? They should be reported to the rangers. Someone might have been hurt!"

"They're long gone. We'd never find them now," Theo replied, squinting into the foliage. "The horses panicking gave them the time they needed to get away. Even if we could go after them, we'd never find them now."

"But who would shoot at—d'you suppose it was robber? This sort of thing never happens in the park! Good Lord, sir, you don't think someone was shooting at you, do you?"

"There were a great many people shooting at me in the war," Theo replied shortly, turning the ball over in his hand. "I had a price on my head for many years." He walked across the pathway and disappeared into the brush on the opposite side. "Someone was lurking over here, you can see where the grass is trampled down and twigs are broken," he called. He turned away, frowning. "He, or they, were waiting for us, it would seem. They seem to have made a sort of nest here for themselves, which would indicate they had been here for a while. Waiting for us, perhaps."

"Why?" Ann asked, her common sense reasserting itself. "Why lurk about? If they meant to rob us, you'd think they'd have done with it. Do you really believe someone means to kill you? Why?"

"Because. No reason, every reason," Theo said half to himself. He peered into the woods then turned. "Perhaps, you know, when one has been hunted, one forever feels hunted. Perhaps some child has filched his father's pistol. Perhaps it was, as you say, a footpad. Or perhaps it was something more. But they are gone now, so it makes no difference." He looked at Ann. "Are you all right?"

"A little shaken, but—oh, look at your face!"

He put a hand to his cheek and looked at it. "Blood," he said.

"So it would seem," Ann replied. She withdrew a handkerchief from her pocket and dabbed at his cheek. "I think you avoided a direct hit, sir," she said. Digging in her reticule, she produced a small mirror, which she held up for his inspection. "It looks like the merest scratch, but a fraction of an inch more and—"

"It must have grazed my cheek," Theo said. "Ah!" He winced. "Careful, I beg of you, Miss Ingersoll!"

"Sorry," Ann said. "I didn't mean to hurt you. You ought to dress that with some Basilicum powder. There! It's stopped bleeding, but really, what in the world—you might have been killed!"

"That may have been precisely the thing," Theo said grimly. "Miss Ingersoll, I must ask you to say nothing of this! There are reasons that I would prefer not to have this discussed!"

I seem to be the keeper of all the secrets, Ann thought.

Aloud she said, "There! It is the merest scratch! If you like, you may tell anyone who asks that you ran beneath a tree branch or something like that."

"Thank you! I hope that driving with you is not always so exciting," he said dryly.

"Still, I think if someone were shooting at me, I would want everyone to know about it. It lessens the chances of a successful assassination, if the murderer knows you know," Ann suggested.

"You are a remarkably self-possessed female," Theo muttered in grudging admiration. "Most young ladies would be shrieking in hysterics or fainting dead away at the mere thought of bloodshed."

"My father says my greatest problem is that I lack sensibility," Ann sighed. She dabbed at his cheek. "I don't know precisely how it should come to be, but I am only shaking a very little bit right now!"

"Brave girl!" the prince said. "Let me hand you back up into the phaeton. I think we should get back to the others now."

"Prince Theodoric, if someone is shooting at you, I think it would be advisable to inform someone! This is England, there are laws here—"

"There are laws in Batavia, too, Miss Ingersoll. And in both countries, there are those who would break those laws. This is no game for a female; I beg you to stay well out of it! I would prefer not to see a lady concerned in this affair!"

"No game for a female! That ball might just as easily hit me as you, sir! I can well understand why someone would want to shoot you! You are odious!" Ann looked straight ahead, gripping the reins firmly in her hands. "Remind me not to drive with you again, sir! I value my own life far too much to jeopardize it in whatever game you are playing!"

"Just as you say, ma'm!" The prince replied grimly. The rest of the ride was accomplished in silence.

Prince Theo's mood was not elevated when they drew up before the West Gate to find his cousin Johannes had joined Colonel Rodney in the prince's curricle, where he seemed very much at his ease.

Johannes, resplendent in a bottle-green waistcoat, breeches of a delicate fawn hue, and a high-crowned beaver, was apparently entertaining in high style. Even Colonel Rodney was allowing himself a thin laugh.

"Look what I found strolling along the Row," he said by way of greeting to the prince as they drew abreast of each other. "He begged to be taken up, and so I did."

"Ah, my dear cousin and the charming Miss Ingersoll!" Johannes announced in ringing tones.

"Were you a naughty boy, dear cousin? It looks as if Miss Ingersoll might have had to defend herself!"

Unconsciously, Theo put a hand up to his cheek. "A chance run-in with a tree branch," he drawled. "You know what women drivers are like! Miss Ingersoll allowed the horses to run away with her."

Ann glared at him furiously, but recalling that she had given her word, she bit her lower lip and said nothing.

"*I* would feel privileged to take a ride beside the charming Miss Ingersoll," Johannes declared, bringing his quizzing glass up to his eye in order to survey Ann. "Quite a turnout!"

"So, what brings you to the park?" Theo asked. "I thought you hated fresh air."

"I had the strangest fancy this afternoon to go and take a stroll," Johannes replied airily. "I thought I might enjoy showing off my new waistcoat. It is nice, isn't it?"

Theo looked at it dispassionately. "So, where did you find my cousin?" he asked Colonel Rodney.

"Strolling along the Rose Walk at Rotten Row, ogling all the females," the colonel replied.

"We were on the other side of the Serpentine from you," Theo said meaningfully. "We might have been able to throw a stone across the woods and hit you."

Johannes raised an eyebrow. "Whyever would you want to do that, dear cousin?" he asked blandly. If Theo had given him a turn, he did not show it.

Ann stole a thoughtful glance at the prince.

Prince Theo frowned. "I hate to cut this short, but I am engaged to dine at the Russian Embassy tonight, so I must reclaim my curricle. Miss Ingersoll, I must thank you for a most interesting expedition."

"Please don't forget me, Miss Ingersoll!" Johannes said. "I am going your way!"

"You don't even know where I'm going," Ann countered.

"It matters not. Anything is better than this walking you English are so fond of," Johannes sighed. "Good day; Colonel Rodney!"

"I think it best for you to come with me, cousin," Theo said heavily.

An odd look passed over Johannes's face; his expression contorted from a soigné charmer into an angry, resentful child. It lasted but a second, and then his composure was restored, but in that moment, Ann noted the depth of his rancor for his cousin.

"But my dear Theo, whatever it is, it can wait," he said smoothly, smiling at Ann. "I can't disappoint a lady, and I do so want to ride with such a credible whip as Miss Ingersoll." So saying, he descended from the curricle and cast himself up into Ann's phaeton, where he assumed an attitude of great ease.

"I would be happy to drop you off wherever you chose to go," Ann said, feeling that she had no choice. Joseph took his position on the jump behind her seat, staring straight ahead.

"Best not to keep the horses standing, Miss," he said expressionlessly.

The group made their farewells and Ann guided her team out of the park and into the street.

Johannes adjusted his hat. "Ah, there is Lady Jersey!" he said as they passed that lady's barouche.

Her ladyship waved and smiled at Johannes, staring with open curiosity at Ann.

"You do not know the estimable Lady Jersey?" he asked Ann when they had passed her.

"I know her. She knows who I am," Ann replied briefly.

"But she is not friend to you?"

"No."

"She is a patroness of Almack's. I would think that you would be most anxious to know such an important lady."

Ann threw him a sideways glance. "Not particularly. I have no desire to go to Almack's, and even if I did, I would not be issued a voucher."

"Oh?"

"My father is in Trade, Count. By the lights of the Upper Ten Thousand, that places me quite beyond the pale."

"I see," Johannes said thoughtfully. He leaned back against the seat, to all intents and purposes a man with abundant leisure, enjoying the balmy weather and the company. "Forgive me, Miss Ingersoll, if I seem impertinent, but I am a stranger in your country, and English ways are new to me."

"My erstwhile mentor, Miss Ridgely, always says that one learns by asking."

"You tell me that the aristocracy and the mercantile classes do not mix. And yet, you and Lady Louisa are on excellent terms."

"Yes. We went to school together."

"And the duke and duchess, they permit this?"

"Their Graces have been very kind to me. And I

like them very much. And my father and the duke have become friendly."

"I do not see."

"There is nothing to see, count," Ann said a little more shortly than she intended. "I am quite happy with my life. I do not seek entree into fashionable society. In fact, I agree with my father's opinion that fashionable society is both decadent and frivolous."

"Ah!" the count murmured. "I think I understand. You believe, as I do, that people should rise on their own merits."

"Well, yes, I suppose I do," Ann agreed. "Now that you put it that way."

He seemed to think for a moment. His next question surprised her. "And what do you think about Lady Louisa marrying my cousin?"

"What is there to think? It is between them, don't you agree? I think Louisa would make an excellent crown princess. She has been trained from birth to occupy a high station."

"And yet, she and Colonel Rodney are *les cousins*."

"Distant cousins."

"They seem sincerely attached to each other."

"They have known each other since birth."

"And yet," Johannes repeated thoughtfully, touching a finger to his chin, "it does not seem to me to be a relationship like that of family."

Ann shrugged. "Perhaps in other circumstances, things would have been different."

"Ah, Miss Ingersoll, I believe you have a romantic heart."

"You are quite mistaken, Count. I have no heart for romance at all. I believe in women's rights, you see."

"Ah! A feminist! Most admirable! For my part, I have always thought females to be the stronger sex. But women's rights do not preclude romance, you know."

"They do for me," Ann said firmly.

"A great pity," Johannes sighed. "My mother was a most intelligent woman. A very strong woman, with great stamina. Vast insight. And yet, she had the heart to marry my father, and they lived together most amiably, united in their belief that they were more suited to rule Batavia than my late uncle."

"Oh?" Ann replied, fascinated by this brief glimpse into the family life of the von Hazloe clan. "Alas, unlike your mother, I have found no gentleman with whom I think I could live most amiably, as you say."

"I think perhaps you will find differently, in time," he said airily. "Ah, Miss Ingersoll, I hope to have the pleasure of seeing you again! You must save me a dance, if not at Almack's, at the Duchess of Coldstone's ball!" He smiled his most charming smile. "You may put me down here, you please! I am only a block from the Residence, and that is not such a long walk, even for me!"

With that, he was gone, leaving Ann to stare after him, half-intrigued, half-irritated, and completely and unreasonably charmed.

6

"*I can't like it,* Miss Ann," Jeremy Briggs said dolefully. "It seems to me that if your father wants you to entertain his business friends at home, he ought to have some respectable female to bear you company."

The urge to kill the messenger surged through Ann, although it was inspired more by a dislike of the bearer of tidings than the note he had just handed her. With an unerring instinct, Mr. Briggs had found precisely the wrong thing to say, then said it.

Ann looked up at Mr. Briggs, not bothering to conceal her annoyance. "What? And have my Aunt Wigglesworth living here? For you know that she is my only relation who meets the necessary qualifications to be my chaperone; all the rest of my female relations have husbands or families to take up their attentions. Since she and my father have ever been at cross crabs, I doubt that would work. Besides, she would never leave Bath and her horrible pug dogs to come to London! I thank you very much for your concern, Mr. Briggs, but as you well know, ever since I put up my hair and let down my skirts, I have served as my father's hostess without undue mishap."

She looked down at the hastily scrawled note again. If only her father wrote in a fist as comprehensible as his clerks'! It seemed to tell her to expect a guest for dinner, but for the life of her, she could not make out the name. She squinted at it, turning the paper this way and that to see if she could decipher it.

"Even so, Miss Ann, speaking as one who has your best interests at heart, I cannot help but feel that I must speak!"

Ann's eyebrows went up. "Whatever is there to speak about, Mr. Briggs?" she asked in a tone that would have warned a more sensitive person of impending danger.

Jeremy Briggs, however, was oblivious to such nuances. Genius he might be at business, his skills in normal social intercourse were almost nonexistent. Perceiving an opportunity, he pressed ahead with his opinions. "One cannot feel that your excursions into fashionable society have seduced you into false hopes!" he said dolefully.

"False hopes of what?" Ann asked absently. A guest for dinner, yes, she understood that much, and was not discommoded with that news. Mr. Ingersoll frequently brought home business guests, and she was prepared to do her part to be certain they were attended to with good hospitality, then retire discreetly with the arrival of the port to allow business to continue. Who was this guest her father was bringing home? A Mr. Prong? Pring? Pringle? She could not make out the crucial word, scrawled as it was in what appeared to be Arabic. If only her father wrote a clear fist!

"False hopes of rising above your station in life! I know that you may well dream of becoming a peeress or some such thing, but please allow one whose knowledge of the world is somewhat larger than your own to drop a hint into your ear!"

"What?" Ann asked, her attention finally caught by Mr. Briggs. "What peeress? Has Father invited a peeress to dinner? Why ever would he do that?"

"My concern is for your happiness, of course!" Mr. Briggs continued, bound upon his own course of thought, much to Ann's bewilderment. Mr. Briggs was not a great one to listen to others. "But it is not meant, can never be meant to happen! Such ambitions are illusive! They can only end in your disappointment or worse! Far worse, Miss Ann, for these fashionable fellows are an immoral lot, and like as not to take advantage of females like yourself!"

Puzzled, Ann shook her head. Then resentment and amusement struggled in her breast, and amusement won. "Are you trying to tell me something?" she asked Mr. Briggs, opening her eyes very wide.

"Accept the guidance of one who wishes you well!" Mr. Briggs exclaimed. "Nothing good can come of association with the fashionable fribbles of the ton!"

It was on the tip of Ann's tongue to inform Mr. Briggs that she was not in the habit of associating with fashionable fribbles of the ton, much less pinning any marital hopes on a peer, but she decided such denials were wasted on this blockhead, and determined to listen him out, hoping to be rid of him that much sooner. "Oh, Mr. Briggs," she said, suppressing her laughter with supreme effort. "I am so thankful for your advice, for now that I have heard you out, I must cast aside all hopes of ever marrying a peer. Only tell me who this peeress is that my father is dining with, and we shall call everything even!"

His thin chest puffed out self-importantly. "There! I thought a word in your ear would do you a world of good," he said, much pleased with himself. "But still, one cannot condone your going into the quagmire known as the fashionable world," he added. "My dear mother was saying to me only the other day that no good ever comes of looking higher than our own station in life for our happiness."

Thinking of that joylessly pious female, whose scriptural studies seemed entirely given over to finding justification for her own selfishness and damnation for those who disagreed with her, Ann had to sigh. Not for the first time, she pitied Mr. Briggs's spinster sisters, whose lives were entirely given over to catering to their mother's many imaginary illnesses, living out their days in a dark and cramped house in Camden Town that smelled of cats and medicine. One brief visit there many years ago had decided her against another.

"Yes, yes of course," Ann said, certain that no further information on the coming guest would be pried out of the clerk, who was working himself into a state that she was beginning to find annoying beyond her capacity for civility. "Thank you for bringing my father's note around to me. Now, if you will excuse me, I must consult with Addle and Cook on changes in tonight's menu—"

"Miss Ann!" Jeremy Briggs exclaimed. "Finding you thus alone, I must needs speak!"

Ann glanced around the drawing room, as if hoping to see company there she had previously not discerned. "Please don't," she sighed, when she saw there was no escape. "You will only cause us both a great deal of odious embarrassment and—"

"I *must* speak! I cannot remain silent!" As he spoke, he grasped Ann's hands in his own. His skin felt like dry old paper.

"Mr. Briggs, you embarrass both of us," Ann said, becoming more impatient. She tried to withdraw her hands but he held her tightly. The clock on the mantel chimed seven, as if to remind Ann that there was very little time to waste.

"Miss Ann! Please allow me to speak to your father!" Mr. Briggs implored her. "You must know that I have long cherished the hope, the very great hope that you would consent to—"

"Please, Mr. Briggs! Don't say anything that will cause either one of us embarrassment," Ann sighed, struggling to release her hands from his grip.

"I must speak! I must! You know that your father cannot live forever, and that someone must run his business and manage his affairs—"

"Mr. Briggs! *Please*!" Ann protested. "My father

is hale and hearty, and I could never, ever marry you!"

"Miss Ann, please—only think of the future of Ingersoll Limited!"

"Oh, this is outside of enough! It is clear now! Ingersoll Limited is what you love, not me! Mr. Briggs, if you do not unhand me, I will have to hurt you!" Ann exclaimed. "You are behaving in a most odious manner!"

The sound of Addle clearing his throat interrupted whatever Mr. Briggs was about to say next. The old butler's face was a mask of disinterested professionalism as he opened the drawing room doors.

"The Prince of Batavia," Addle announced in a dispassionate voice, and stood aside for that gentleman to pass into the room.

"*You!*" Ann breathed.

It would have been hard to tell who was more surprised. Miss Ingersoll, rendered nonplused after her initial outburst, simply stared, a dark flush building in her cheeks. Surprise, embarrassment, and something that looked a great deal like anger flickered across her face as she moved hastily away from Mr. Briggs.

Theo's eyebrows rose as he scanned this interesting tableau. What might have been a smile flickered briefly across his features before being replaced by a professionally neutral expression. "Mr. Briggs was just leaving, Addle," Ann said stiffly, recovering herself with what she hoped was an admirable grace.

"As you say, Miss," Addle replied, holding the door open for the stunned clerk, who looked as if he wanted to throttle the prince.

With no other choice, the frustrated clerk adjusted his spectacles and stalked out, throwing a dark look at the prince. Utterly impassive, Addle shut the door behind him, leaving Ann and Theo to stare at each other. It was a long, uncomfortable moment before either could speak.

"*You* are the daughter of Mr. David Ingersoll?" Theo asked, astonished. He might, he reflected, have known, the way his luck had been running lately, but in the press of business, it had never occurred to him to put the two together.

"Yes! Ingersoll Wines and Spirits Limited! And you are—" Ann squinted at the note, now sadly crumbled from being held in her hand while she was fending off Mr. Briggs's offense. "Not a peeress, nor a Mr. Prong—oh! I see now. It's *Prince*! Prince Theodoric! Oh dear! My father's handwriting leaves a great deal to be desired at times! His great, scrawling fist, you see, he writes as fast as he thinks and he thinks so very swiftly—" In a bout of anxiety, the words came tumbling foolishly out. "I didn't expect— that is, I didn't know that you would be coming—"

This exposure to a flustered and embarrassed, altogether more *human* Miss Ingersoll deflected the prince's initial sense of having been handed an unpleasant surprise. Her cheeks were flushed, her eyes were light, and her breast rose and fell with her breathing. It was not unbecoming to her, he thought a bit wildly.

To his own surprise, Theo suppressed the sarcastic remark that he might have tossed given this opportunity. Impulsively, he reached out and tucked an errant curl behind her ear. "You know," he said in a voice far more gentle than he had ever expected to hear himself use with her, "we do seem to meet in the oddest predicaments, Miss Ingersoll."

He had expected her to laugh and toss it off with one of her abrupt sallies. Instead she pressed her hands against her flaming cheeks. "I must speak to the servants! We had such a short notice that we were to entertain tonight—my father should really have told me earlier—if you will make yourself comfortable, I shall tell Addle to bring you a glass of Madeira, and I shall be back instantly! Excuse me!"

And with that, she fled the room, leaving Theo to stare after her, frowning thoughtfully. He caught a glimpse of himself in the mirror over the mantel and shook his head. "So that fellow is the one who's captured the virago's heart," he said to his reflection. "Dull sort, but perhaps that's what she likes."

After giving quick orders to Addle, Ann fled up the stairs to her own room. Of all the guests her father could possibly have invited, she thought distractedly, pulling the pins out of her sadly disarranged hair. But of course, it all made sense; Ingersoll Wines and Spirits Limited was the largest importer of champagne in England and the colonies; the Prince of Batavia was visiting on a trade mission to sell his country's national product. But to allow the man to find her in *such* a position! It was not only humiliating to be caught again fending off unwanted attentions from a man, but it made her look as if she were fast, which she most assuredly was not! Curse the luck! She who believed she had never attracted more than a passing interest from any man, to find herself not once, but twice the victim of unwelcome attentions—and to have both instances witnessed by the one person who would be most likely to draw the wrong conclusions!

Fumbling with her hair, Ann's mind raced, and it took all of her self-control to keep her hands from shaking with her anger. *Damn* that fool Jeremy Briggs, for choosing that moment to create his scene, his very *embarrassing* scene! His love was not for her, of course, but for Ingersoll Wines and Spirits Limited! The man was not only a troll, but a troll with no address, no manners, and no hope! As repulsive as he was, he was even more repulsive for telling her that his true passion was her inheritance! No woman, not even a feminist, likes to think she is not loved for herself rather than her expectations! Angrily, she ran a hairbrush through her curls and quickly pinned her hair back into place. Of course, being Jeremy Briggs, he had to choose specially the wrong thing to say and precisely the wrong way in which to say it, at exactly the wrong time. No doubt about it, this time she would have to speak to her father about the clerk's unwelcome attentions. He might see Mr. Briggs as the ideal son-in-law, but really! And in front of the prince, too! Not, of course, that she cared a whit what he thought, but still, well, really! It was all too much. And she would have something to say to Father, too, for not giving her more notice. There was only the two capons, a roast of beef, and four or five removes for dinner, and he would think that she set a poor table. And the wines! He would of course be looking very closely at the wines they served; wines were his business, if a prince could be said to be in business. Well, at least she would trust the unflappable Addle to venture into the cellars and get down a bottle of the good '91 port and a better year of claret than the usual stuff they drank *en famille* . . .

Suddenly, she paused, the hairbrush halfway raised to her head, staring at herself in the mirror as if beholding her image for the first time. Why was she in such a flap over a man she didn't even like? she wondered. Prince or no prince, he had shown himself to be quite human. There was no need to impress him, any more than any other business relation of her father's, save that she was determined to show this prince that the Ingersolls might be in trade, but they were every bit as genteel as the Coldstones. And why? He needed the goodwill of Ingersoll Ltd. far more than the Ingersolls needed him. Still, she could not help but be vaguely aware of a confusion of feelings. But this was not the time for self-examination. Prince or no prince, the man was a guest in her home, and deserved the most basic civility commanded by hospitality. Her humor reasserted itself, and she smiled, shaking her head. "Foolishness," she told herself, thinking what a wonderful story it would make when she told it to Louisa.

There was no need to pinch color into her cheeks; they were still glowing. She twisted before the pier glass and surveyed herself critically. Her dinner dress was of iris-colored satin, décolleté, with ivory slashed and faggoted sleeves and a deeply banded hem of ivory and silver lozenges. It was, she noted with relief, not too sadly crushed by Mr. Briggs's inopportune predations. Long kid gloves and a handsome pearl and diamond parure completed her toilette. She picked up a Norwich shawl from the chair, took a deep breath and fled the room just her abigail appeared in the doorway.

Miss Keating's mouth was an O of astonishment. "Oh, Miss, is it true that the master's got a real prince home for dinner?" she asked, automatically smoothing the pleats in Ann's dress and professionally draping her shawl about her shoulders, "You really shouldn't try to dress yourself, Miss Ann, that's what I'm here for," she sniffed. "If I'd known you was to sit down with a prince tonight, I've had laid out your lovely celestial blue with the lace, the one you wore to Lady Louisa's—"

"No, no, this is fine," Ann said quickly, adding, "And he's only the prince of a very small country, Keating, so it doesn't really signify! Alderman Wellborne, who comes to dine with us regularly, is far more important, you know!"

Nonetheless, as she bustled quickly down the stairs again, she had the distinct feeling that all the housemaids would somehow or another contrive by the end of the night to catch a glimpse of the famous guest.

"I took the liberty of serving His Highness the Chartres '04 Madeira," Addle informed her as she descended. "I have also instructed Cook to prepare a lobster as a first remove, and to add a turtle soup to the first course. I have decanted a bottle of the '91 port, and taken up a bottle of the '11 claret and the '09 Rhine-Mossel hock to serve with the second and third courses." He cleared his throat. "I also thought it best to chill a bottle of the '15 Champagne Batavia for dessert, which will be raspberry tart, fruit, and cheese."

"Addle, you are a genius," Ann said gratefully.

The butler inclined his head with a small smile. "Don't worry about a thing, Miss Ann. The prince will dine as well as he would in a duke's household. Better, perhaps."

She found the prince in the drawing room, seated before a pleasant fire with a glass of Madeira in hand. Theo was gazing at the portrait of her late mother which hung above the mantelpiece. He rose when she entered the room, and she noted that he was in well-tailored evening dress, with only a miniature on his left breast to display his rank.

"The lady is your mother?" he asked, indicating the Romney painting. "She is lovely."

Ann nodded. "My late mother. She died when I was very small, but by all accounts she was very pretty. I take after my father, I fear."

"Not in all ways. You have your mother's eyes, you know. May I pour you a glass of your very fine Madeira?"

"Please. My father will be here in a few minutes. Sometimes when traffic is heavy in the City, he is delayed in coming home, for which I apologize."

"No, it is I who should apologize," Theo replied, handing her a glass of wine. "In my country, when an invitation is issued for seven, it means seven. In England, an invitation for seven means promptly at eight. I went to school here, I should know better. But

I have no secretary with me, as you see." He smiled sheepishly. "How very welcoming your house is. Elegant, yet comfortable! This is what I should like to do with my apartments at the palace." He made a face. "The previous occupants helped themselves to a great many of the furnishings, you see!"

He held up his glass and Ann touched the rim with her own. They both drank, and Ann considered this. What would she do if she and her father were thrown out of the only house she had ever known, only to return and find it looted of all the dear, familiar things?

"I trust no one else has shot at you?" she asked, not in jest.

He shook his head. "No. I think it must have been an accident. Pray don't think about it. I don't! Is that a Fragonard over there?" Theo asked quickly. "You have some very fine pictures here. I was particularly entranced with that Italian landscape in the hall. . . ."

"My father will be pleased that you have noticed his pictures. Art is quite an interest of his. I think he's disappointed that I have exhibited so little talent in that direction, but I can at least appreciate the gifts of others. Should you like to see the pictures?"

"Of course," Theo said. "I should enjoy that very much."

"The Duke of Coldstone says Papa's eye for painting is very good, much better than his," Ann said, leading the prince through the rooms. "And it's nothing to the collection at Coldstone Castle, but Father loves his Italian Primitives, which you may see in the Green Salon. Louisa is quite a talented watercolorist. Unfortunately, it is not one of my talents. Everything I do turns to mud on the page. Now, this is a Cosmic—"

In this manner, he was able to distract her from further questions on stray pistol shots or the Coldstone family, neither subject being one he wished to discuss.

When Mr. Ingersoll came in, he found his daughter extolling the virtues of the painter Turner to a somewhat dubious Theo. "But just look at the sky," she was saying.

"Ah, Prince! I see you are being entertained by my daughter. You'll forgive my delay, I hope; the evening traffic out of the City gets worse every year; a press of men, horses, and carriages such as you've never seen," Mr. Ingersoll said, putting out his hand for the prince, who shook it firmly. "Ann, have you made sure our guest has a glass of—good! Good. Your Highness, may I present you to my daughter?"

"I have had the honor of Miss Ingersoll's acquaintance for almost a fortnight," Theo said with a little smile at Ann. "We were introduced by the Duchess of Coldstone."

"Ah," Mr. Ingersoll said. "My daughter moves in society; I do not, as you know. Her Grace has been quite kind to my girl." He too smiled fondly on Ann. "Goes to every fashionable rig and row in town, don't you?"

"Not every one," Ann replied lightly. A lesser female might have blanched to hear her father address a prince in such a blunt manner, but Ann slipped her hand into her father's arm and leveled a gray-eyed look at Theo, daring him to look down at her parent for being in Trade and being who he was, without the grand manner of the ton.

She need not have worried about Theo. In their afternoon summit, he had developed a great liking for Mr. Ingersoll, and a great appreciation for his knowledge of wines. He found the wine nabob's common sense and forthrightness a great relief after his dealings with the Upper Ten Thousand's rigid manners. In society, he might swim in treacherous waters; when it came to dealing with the business of champagne, Theo felt himself to be on very solid ground. Another in his position might have sent equerries and envoys to deal with the business of selling champagne. But Batavia could not afford such a staff. Besides, no one would know the trade as well as one who was raised up in it. And in that sense, he was as much a man of business as David Ingersoll.

He wondered if she were ashamed of her father and her origins in a family in Trade, and thought if she were, it lessened her, not Mr. Ingersoll.

Soon the two men were deep in discussion about tariffs, export taxes, and noble rot. It was clear to Ann that there was no need for her to do more than look interested as they bargained over the costs of importing Champagne Batavia to England and debated the merits of German and Spanish wines, the problems of shipping and transport, and the marketing of a superior product to a country hungry for luxury after the deprivations of the long war.

"In short, the first year, I think we can sell upwards of thirty tuns in London alone. In the provinces, less, perhaps, but if we can make our job-bers in the North and the Midlands see that Champagne Batavia is far superior to the French product, well, sir, we can write our own ticket in four years. And there's also the colonial market."

"True. One thing we haven't discussed yet is importing spirits into Batavia. I think there could be a small market for West Indies rum, and a larger one for British ales and beers, which are some of the finest in the world, to my way of thinking. As you know, we must import most of our corn from France and the German states, so making beers is not economically advantageous for us. We've been used to importing our beers from Westphalia and Hesse, but I can see a balance here—"

"—that would prove advantageous to Batavia in any trade agreement. True, very true! Well, I've got a man at the Foreign Office who can work with your people to smooth the way, but unless we get into another war, I can't see much that would signify—"

And so the conversation went, all through the evening. Ann turned her thoughts inward while the two men debated the rival merits of the Troiel and Ste-Juste vineyards, oblivious to the way in which the staff flickered around the perimeters of the room, attempting to catch a glimpse of their illustrious visitor.

She was relieved to excuse herself when Addle removed the covers and set the port and cigars on the table.

"I'll leave you gentlemen to your business conversation," Ann said with just the faintest trace of irony. They barely noticed her exit.

"Who would have thought that an aristocrat would know so much, so very much about the actual process of making wine?" she wondered as she settled back in the drawing room by the fire to sip a solitary cup of coffee and peruse a new novel she had gotten that day from Mudie's Lending Library. "Only think of the Prince Regent or his brothers attempting to discourse from experience on British industry," she thought. Poor Louisa, what a dull life she was in for, if he expected her to take an interest in anything more than the drinking of champagne, and only a sip at that!

She was just about to pour herself a cup of coffee when Addle opened the doors. "Lady Louisa is calling, Miss. If I may say so, she seemed somewhat distraught when I informed her that His Highness was dining here tonight." He cleared his throat. "I took the liberty of escorting her up the back stairs to your bedroom, the other servants all being engaged in various duties in the vicinity of the dining room."

Ann rose to her feet, astonished. "Lady Louisa here? At this hour? But—"

"She was escorted by Colonel Rodney. He's sitting in the carriage outside. I thought that might attract less attention." Addle remained impassive. Bonaparte himself might have appeared at the door, and the butler would not have turned a hair.

"I shall go up to her. Can you keep the prince and my father in the dining room a while longer?"

"I have taken the liberty of decanting the Viejallo '03 port and replenishing the cigarillos," Addle replied, his tone implying his great hurt that she would think he had not anticipated this necessity.

"Addle, you are a genius," Ann repeated.

He inclined his head and moved with a stately tread toward the dining room, where great clouds of smoke were hazing the atmosphere. He scattered two of the downstairs maids who were peering at the prince through the crack in the double doors and entered the room.

In her boudoir, Ann found Louisa, in evening dress, anxiously pacing the rug. "Oh, thank God you are here!" she exclaimed when Ann walked in. "I am in the most terrible tangle, Ann, and I know not what to do. Mama thinks I am at the Torringtons' drum!"

"Then what are you doing here and why is Randolph Rodney sitting in a carriage outside?" Ann asked. "And don't you know that the prince is downstairs at port and cigars with my father?"

Louisa stopped pacing and stared at Ann. "What shall we do?" she squeaked.

"The pair of them have been boring me senseless with talk about champagne all night long! I now know more than I want to know about trade agreements and vineyards and noble rot, believe me!"

"Yes, yes, of course," Louisa said. She shook her head. "I have no luck, none at all! Oh, Ann what are we to do? I can't face him, not now, not like this!" She grasped her friend's hands. "Only fancy, Ann! Last night, we were at the Ombersleys', and Randolph and I went to supper together, and over the ices, I declared myself to him. And I found out he feels the same way!"

"Oh!" Ann said. "How wonderful for you—or is it?" A sudden, depressing thought hit her. "But what about your parents? And what about the prince?"

Louisa sank into the chaise, crushed. "There you have it!" she sighed. "My parents would never, *ever* allow me to marry Randolph!

"Especially not when they are expecting the prince to speak to Papa! And Randolph says that he could never betray his great friend Theo! He says that that would be above all things wrong, and that we must learn to live without one another!"

"While one can see his point, it is excessively annoying for him to feel that way," Ann sighed. "When it was Randolph who suggested the match between the you and the prince in the first place! Well, I suppose there can be no harm in telling you now that he has been carrying the torch for you since he came back from the wars and you were no longer his gawky awkward cousin but a lovely woman. While one must admire him for being honorable, it is still rather annoying. You don't suppose he could be convinced to speak to the prince about all this?"

"No! He feels it would be dishonorable!"

"Silly! It's as plain as a pikestaff that the prince doesn't care about you any more than you care about him! I am very glad that I am not from a family where one has to make an alliance rather than a marriage!"

"The prince is a very nice man, and I daresay if it were not for Randolph, I could marry him and we should deal extremely well together. But—"

"I quite understand. The thing of it is, Prince Theodoric must marry and create an heir, and I think that he really doesn't care who he marries as long as it's someone who's good for his country. So, why should he feel distress if you tell him you don't want to marry him?"

"Mama and Papa," Louisa said simply.

"There is that," Ann agreed. "No mean obstacle."

"I really think if it weren't for the prince, eventually they would have allowed me to marry Randolph. He is family, in a way, his grandmother having been born a Coldstone," Louisa pointed out. "For them, family is much better than royalty. We are planning to go to Coldstone, for a house party, where Papa expects the prince shall ask for my hand." Then she lifted her chin. "Well, I won't marry him. The prince, I mean! I *will* marry Randolph!"

Love, whatever else it had done for Louisa, seemed to have invested her with a will of her own.

"But if you think your parents won't consent, how will you marry him?" Ann asked, "Have you thought of a way to convince them?"

"Never in a thousand years! No, Ann, listen!" Louisa put her hand on her friend's arm. "I mean to elope!"

"*Elope?*" Ann exclaimed, horrified. "Louisa, you can't!"

Louisa thrust out her chin. "Yes, I can. And I will! You watch me! All my life, so far, I've done everything precisely the way Mama and Papa wanted me to, but for the rest of my time on earth, no! I want to spend it with someone I love and care for and trust!"

"What does Randolph say to all of this?" Ann asked.

Louisa shot her a sideways glance. "He says it

won't work. Not only does he feel it's dishonorable, he says that a half-pay officer who lives in the Albany and works on government missions is not the man to support a duke's daughter! But I'll make him see the light, I know I will! I'll seduce him! Then he'll have to elope with me!"

"You can't elope! Only think of the scandal! It would upset your parents so much! Louisa, what has come over you? You're like a different person!"

Louisa turned flashing eyes on her friend and smiled. "I'm in love and he loves me. And I've loved him forever, Ann, you know that! Oh, I know eloping is beyond the pale, but all my life Ann, I've stayed within the rules and where has it gotten me?

"I don't want to go and live in a palace! I'd rather live in a cottage with Randolph! We have some adorable cottages on the estate, you know, with thatched roofs and I could raise chickens and milk a cow, and have a little garden—"

"And I daresay you would hate it within an hour of his carrying you over the threshold! Thatch is full of rats, for one thing, and for another, chickens are amazingly stupid, and while I would dearly love to see you milk a cow, I don't think you'd like that one bit, either. Besides, gardening is hard, dirty work! Manure! You have to use manure in gardening, you know."

"How do you know so much about the country? You were born and raised in London!"

"I've been in the country, you goose! Louisa, you would *hate* being poor, believe me! It's not what you were raised to, and I can't believe Randolph is so crackbrained as to allow you to think of such a thing!"

"Well, he does rather agree with you that it just won't work," Louisa admitted. "But you know when Mama and Papa get used to the idea, there can be a settlement and everything can be worked out. You know that they can't stay angry at me for long. And they do like Randolph. Oh, Ann, can't you talk to Randolph and make him understand that we should head for the border tonight?"

Ann shook her head. "Even if I agreed with you, which I don't, I doubt very much that Randolph would do such a thing! Louisa, it's a crackbrained idea."

"But it's all we have!" Louisa cried.

"There must be something better," Ann said. She rose. "You must leave and go home before your mother notices you are missing! Worse still, the prince and my father might leave their port and catch you here!"

"Well, the prince is a perfectly nice man, but Ann, I don't wish to be a princess! Why don't you marry him?"

"Don't be silly," Ann snapped. "I am not going to marry anyone, especially Prince Theodoric. I don't even much like the man!"

"Someone has to marry him," Louisa said. "Listen! Isn't that your father?"

"Oh, Lord! They must have come out of the drawing room! How am I going to get you out of the house without them seeing you?"

"I'll go down the back stairs," Louisa said quickly,

rising from the chaise where she had thrown herself. "But tell me, Ann what are we going to do?"

"What do you mean we? Louisa, you can't drag me into this!"

But Ann knew that she was already in over her head.

Louisa smiled. "I have an idea," she said. "Suppose that the prince did something incredibly rude. Something that would be sure to offend Papa and Mama, which isn't really hard, you know, they're *such* high sticklers! Something like challenging you to race your phaeton against him for an enormous wager? You know that they cannot abide gaming, after the enormous amounts grandpapa lost! If they thought that the prince was a hardened gamester, they would be sure to look askance at him! Then Mama and Papa would to listen to Randolph's suit, if only because they would be so offended with the prince. And you know you can make him angry enough to do it, Ann. You have the most amazing way of setting his back up."

"Challenge the prince to a race for an enormous wager? Louisa, what sort of a scandal do you want me to make of myself?" Ann demanded, laughing. "It would be one thing to race, but quite another to make a huge wager! Besides, I value your parents' friendship! They have been quite kind to me, you know."

"Well, it's not as if you've never cut a caper, Ann," Louisa said reasonably. "And Papa and Mama will see it as all being the prince's fault. Besides, you never cared what people said about you before."

"Yes, I suppose you are right. Still, I can't like it. Who do you think I am, Letty Lade?"

"There can be no harm in it. You're always saying that females should be able to do anything men do! Besides, Miss Ridgely taught us to meet any challenge!"

Ann blinked. "Well," she said, "I don't think I could do that. Father would kill me dead! But, the prince owes me a match," she added thoughtfully. She knew her grays could best his chestnuts, but still. "This is the most ridiculous idea—"

Louisa threw her arms around Ann. "I knew you would help us!"

"Ann! Ann! Where is the girl?" Mr. Ingersoll's voice, pleasantly rosy with the effects of fine port and good cigars, drifted up the staircase. The gentlemen had emerged from the dining room.

"Down the back stairs," Ann commanded.

Louisa drew her evening cloak about her. "Dear, dear Ann! Thank you so much!" she whispered.

"This is, without a doubt, the *stupidest* thing I've ever undertaken in my life!" Ann muttered, pausing only to be sure Louisa was well on her way out before heading down the front staircase with a stiff smile pasted firmly in place. "An evening that begins with Jeremy Briggs and ends by trying to trick a prince is an evening to remember!"

Mr. Ingersoll and the prince were just settling down in the drawing room when Ann bustled in, slightly out of breath.

Both gentlemen were rather as full as could hold of port and camaraderie; evidently their sampling of several bottles of rare old Oporto had increased their mutual understanding as well as the bloom in their cheeks.

"Ah, here is my daughter," Mr. Ingersoll said jovially. "We were beginning to think you despaired of us and had gone to bed."

"My fault entirely," the prince said apologetically. "When it comes to talking about wine, I am liable to drone on for hours. But when I meet a gentleman so full of knowledge about every aspect of wine, well, you may imagine! My apologies for leaving you in solitary splendor, Miss Ingersoll!"

"I never thought to meet a fella who could tell, just by a sniff of the cork, a Jermiad '03 from a Helios '98! Man's got an amazing nose! A genius at wine, my dear prince, a genius!"

Theo graciously bowed in Mr. Ingersoll's direction. "It is I who should thank you for giving me the opportunity to sample so many fine and diverse ports! Never have I been privileged to sample a Santo Diego '05 before! I thought it was only a myth, a legend!"

"It would appear that you two have been doing a great deal more than sampling," Ann said, more amused than offended. In an age when gentlemen were known as two, three, or even five bottle men, she was quite used to seeing cheerful wine lovers in their cups.

She pulled the bell cord to summon Addle with the coffee tray, and settled down with what she hoped was a demure and decorous attitude upon the sofa. When she heard the front door open and close, she breathed a sigh of relief. In a moment, Addle, stately as ever, appeared with the coffee tray, followed by a footman carrying the tea table, which he placed in front of Ann, trying to catch a discreet glimpse of the prince. With something of a flourish, Addle placed the coffee tray on the table, bending as he did so to murmur near Ann's ear, "Lady Louisa has safely departed, Miss Ann."

"Thank you, Addle," Ann replied with a deep sincerity. "That will be all, for now."

Shooing the curious footman ahead of him, Addle departed the room.

Ann picked up a Limoges cup and poured from the silver pot. "Cream and sugar, sir?" she asked the prince sweetly. "Or do you prefer it black?"

"Black, please, Miss Ingersoll. As I was saying, Mr. Ingersoll, there is nothing Batavia offers you in terms of the first pressing that would disappoint your clients—"

"Do you go to Coldstone with the duke and duchess?" Ann asked the prince as she handed her father his coffee cup.

"Why, yes I do," Theo replied, a little surprised.

"Then I shall have the pleasure of seeing you there," Ann said demurely, smiling at him beneath her lashes. "How is your coffee, Father?"

"I didn't know you were going to the Castle," Mr. Ingersoll said. "When did that come up?"

"Oh, the duchess just asked me," Ann said quickly. "I forgot to mention it to you, Father. It's all right, isn't it? Just a party, Friday to Monday, and I'll be back in time for the Guild Banquet on Wednesday."

"Very well, then, I've no objection," Mr. Ingersoll

agreed. He selected a pear from the silver dish and peeled it with the pearl-handled knife.

"Will you be taking your team, Prince Theodoric?" Ann asked casually, offering the fruit dish.

"I had planned on it," he replied, selecting a fig. He peeled the skin back, exposing the ripe sections, biting into it with strong white teeth. His eyes never left Ann's.

"I had thought I might take my phaeton," she remarked, holding his gaze.

"Ah," Theo said. He wiped his lips with a napkin. Was there a trace of a smile in his eyes?

"I thought perhaps we might have that race we were discussing the other day," Ann offered. She poured herself a cup of coffee, spooning cream into it until it was pale. She waited a beat while the prince enjoyed his fig, turning the spoon. "We might make it more interesting," she added.

"Interesting idea," the prince agreed. He settled back in his chair. "What did you have in mind?"

"Oh, that would be for you to say, but we can certainly make it interesting," Ann promised. She lifted her cup to her lips. Her gaze met Theo's and she blinked.

"Of that much, I am certain," he said dryly, popping the remainder of the fig into his mouth.

"Since I am utterly certain my grays can beat your chestnuts, I feel as if it would be utterly unjust to wager too highly. Shall we say five hundred guineas?"

"Agreed," the prince said, fortified with the confidence and recklessness that can only come from sampling a great deal of port.

It was fortunate that Mr. Ingersoll was at that moment occupied in mentally calculating the projected price of a case of Champagne Batavia '15 on the British market, for he would have objected in no uncertain terms to his daughter's wager. Mr. Ingersoll had the prejudices of his class where gambling was concerned; like the Duke of Coldstone, he was firmly against anything more hazardous than a game of silver loo. Life, he was fond of saying, was far more likely to be a hazard than any game of chance.

"There is just one thing, Miss Ingersoll," Theo said presently.

"What is that?"

"I hope you are prepared to lose!" He softened these words with his most devastating smile.

"On the contrary," Ann replied coolly. "I am prepared to win. Have another fig, Prince Theodoric, you need to keep up your strength."

"On the contrary, dear lady, I expect that I will achieve my ends with the greatest of ease."

As she handed him the fruit plate, Ann smiled, but inwardly, she reflected that of all the tangles she had gotten herself into, this one had to be the most harebrained! She could almost feel sorry for the prince, if only he weren't so arrogant! She could almost enjoy beating him!

7

The first view of Coldstone Castle had put some visitors rather strongly in mind of a Christmas cake, too alien and exotic to be nestled in the lonely English prospect of the rolling Devonshire hills with its massive, ornate gardens spreading out across the plain and down the slopes.

In addition to being colder and damper inside than out, Coldstone Castle always smelled faintly of mildew and old clothes, an essence attributable to a plethora of ancient tapestries that had hung in the Great Hall since commissioned by Hunulf the Unclean, an ancestor who was, unfortunately, not lost in the mists of time, but graphically depicted there in various acts of violence against animals and enemies alike.

Since these were of great antiquity, they always attracted a crowd on Public Days and were written up in many visitors' guides. The public, like the Prince of

Batavia, also was invited to admire and wonder at the Minstrels' Gallery, the Armorial Hall, the Portrait Gallery, the picture collection, the State Rooms, the Queen's Bedroom (used by Queen Elizabeth during a week-long visit with her entourage that nearly bankrupted the second duke), the muniment room, the library, the music room, a series of ducal collections of rocks and minerals, stuffed animals, birds' eggs, weaponry ancient and modern, and a giant ball of string procured over the lifetime of the decidedly eccentric eighth duke, which, for some unknown reason, occupied a room of its own in one of the towers, where it was a prime favorite with the children.

Coldstone Castle had not been used as a fortress since the days of Cromwell, and even by then, it had undergone many renovations and reconstructions under its Tudor owners, made newly rich by fortuitous expeditions into the Spanish Main. All that was left of the original stronghold were four crenellated towers and the keep. Succeeding dukes had each added their own innovations, but none of them had given much thought to the comfort of the occupants.

All of this and much more Prince Theodoric learned on his first day as a guest of the duke. Up one creaking staircase and down another that very august gentlemen led him, through a warren of corridors and hallways, all the while expounding on the history and the outstanding features of the building and its furnishings. If pride were a fire, the prince thought, shivering, this old place would be an equatorial paradise. As the duke opened yet another set of double-hung doors, carved by Luke Lightfoot, that led into yet

another set of occasional rooms, Theo smiled his professional, princely smile and tried to ignore the
chilblains creeping through his extremities.

For the Coldstones, the drafts that whistled down
the stone passageways were considered nice and brac-
ing, and the damp that penetrated the state bedrooms
was ignored in favor of their illustrious occupancy by
notable persons of English history. "Now, Your
Highness, when Queen Anne visited us, this was the
chamber she . . ." the duke would say, and with an
effort, Theo would try to appear interested. He understood that the house tour was a part of his initiation
into the rituals of the Coldstones, but oh, how he
yearned for a warm hearth, a toddy, and a hand of
faro!

The present incumbent's grandfather had been on
the Grand Tour and returned to create an Italianate
landscape around the old pile. The result, a melange of
ancient statuary, water gardens, and ruined temples
had featured, in the warmer months, an ornamental
hermit. However, in a fit of economy the duke had let
the hermit and the second pastry chef go, so that now
the little hermitage stood forlorn and empty in the
middle of a lily pond. Nothing had affected the boxwood maze, the rose gardens, or the fountains with a
thousand jets, which banked a shady path that led to
an Eye of Water that was the envy of many another
stately home owner. The duchess was a passionate
gardener. That is to say, she supervised a dour Scots
genius and a small army of laborers who actually did
the work, since a Duchess of Coldstone should never,
ever sink her fair hands into the soil. Nonetheless, all

major designs and decisions were hers, and she could properly take credit for the Spanish borders in the Italian Fountain Gardens and the introduction of the Jan van der Voorst tulip beds along the Grand Promenade.

It was, Prince Theo decided, all rather more grand and far older than his palace in Batavia. He was acutely aware that the purpose of his invitation to visit the castle was not simply to be impressed. His second mission was to inspect and be inspected by The Family, who had appeared from the four corners of England for this event with their spouses, children, and attendants in tow, all of them complacently aware of their own consequence as Coldstones, all of them aware what was due the consequence of the family.

"Dear Lord, the pack of them look alike," Johannes grumbled to his cousin. "Yellow-haired and pale as ghosts!" He had professed to be not at all certain that he wanted to leave the charms of the Metropolis for this uncomfortable bivouac in the wilds of the county. Theo, as he had expected, would brook no rejection.

"I want you where I can keep an eye on you," the prince had informed him firmly, and so, with a gusty sigh, and a secret feeling of relief, for the ladies and his creditors had grown very pressing of late, Johannes had bade his man pack his things for a journey into the wilderness.

"But you needn't expect me to enjoy myself," he added petulantly. Privately, he hoped that some opportunity might arise that would enable him to thrust a spoke into the prince's plans, that is, if no great effort were required on his part to do so. That little episode in the park had been more than a little exhausting; it had been futile, and so he had informed his coconspirator. And it had put Theo on his guard; this, Johannes intuitively understood, although Theo had not discussed the episode with him. Indeed, Johannes sulked, Theo never discussed *anything* with him!

It might have been expected that Johannes would gaze at the wonders offered to him at Coldstone Castle with awe and approbation. But having sampled the good life in the great castles of Europe, he shivered with cold and horror at the food and entertainment that awaited him.

His assigned room was in the Tudor wing of the pile, a darkly paneled chamber with a vast fireplace that choked out smoke and a faint, baby's breath of heat. Wind rattled at the windows and billowed the ancient curtains. The sheets were damp, and the hot water, carried up in cans from the kitchens a quarter-mile away, arrived at a lukewarm temperature. His man, too well trained to complain aloud, still managed to make it clear by his martyred demeanor that his accommodations were not at all what a gentleman's gentleman was used to.

Of a consequence, when Johannes descended to dinner that evening, he felt that he was not at his best; his cravat, usually so masterfully attended to, was imperfect, even after several attempts, and his man had neglected to iron his shoelaces!

After wandering futilely through several long passageways and echoing corridors, he was finally discovered by a sympathetic footman, whose sole occupation was to round up and guide lost guests to their destination. This individual was able to escort him to the State Dining Room, a vast, Arctic chamber with a vaulted ceiling and yet more tapestries and a tiny coal fire in the hearth, where a long table filled with more than a dozen Coldstones, in all their most depressing familial dinner party attire, greeted his eyes.

An enormous silver epèrgne, the size of a garden urn, sat squarely in the middle of the long, long table rather like a giant, misshapen frog. It had been the gift of Louis XIV to the ninth duke, for what reason, no one remembered.

To his horror, Johannes found himself seated between an ancient, imperious and very deaf dowager in a turban and a colorless young cousin in a feathered headdress, who, barely out of the schoolroom, met his conversational gambits with a waterfall of giggles. For a man who lived for good conversation, this was torture, but the worst was yet to come.

The meal, he judged, might have been served at any good sponging house. It started with a thin, jaundice-colored soup, lurched inexorably through seven courses and forty removes in the English style of boiled or charred, all them over- or undercooked to a pastelike tastelessness, ending with overripe cheese, an assortment of desiccated fruits, and a sorbet. Against nature and all odds, in that chilly house, it arrived puddled on his plate.

The port was, to put it politely, indifferent. He was amazed that Theo could swallow it, for his cousin was notoriously fastidious about his wines. The conversation of the gentlemen at the table, the ladies, of course, having withdrawn, was of such an insipidity as to make Johannes feel as if his very teeth hurt. It seemed like an eternity until the duke pushed himself back from the table, asking his guests if they should now join the ladies.

The thought of female company perked up Johannes's spirits. But here again, he was disappointed. The ladies, like the port, had not improved with age. They had been shivering around a meager fire until their flesh looked quite blue in their low-cut evening dresses. They greeted the men with the sort of long-suffering weariness that indicated that they had been kept waiting for their hot coffee far too long.

In the Crimson Drawing Room, one look about at his assembled fellow guests convinced him that a house party at Coldstone Castle would not be as dreadful as he had first thought.

It would be even worse.

There was just something about these Coldstones, all yellow-haired and pale-skinned, that made him feel hipped. Lady Louisa was the belle of the family, but from there, every other female was definitely downhill. Even the in-laws seemed a lusterless lot. There were no flirtatious beauties with whom he could occupy his time, no inveterate gamesters with whom he might wile away the evenings in a game or two of chance, or so it seemed at first impression.

The duchess's evangelical tendencies offended his libertine sensibilities and her horticultural passions left him at a dead bore standstill. He did not know the difference between a cleome and a daffodil and could not have been less interested. The duke's single interest, as far as Johannes could tell, was the history of his own family, and Johannes, whose ancestors had been a colorful and well-ennobled lot, could not have cared less about the bloodlines of a bloodless English duke who seemed, by all accounts, to be a faithful husband, a good father, a fair landlord, and a conscientious member of the House. And, in Johannes's eyes, a dead bore.

When some of the ladies, and the younger men too, begged Lady Louisa to get out her harp and entertain them with some of the dear old ballads, it was all Johannes could do not to scream in terror. "Lachrymose songs, especially those sang by naive virgins, put me to sleep!" he hissed at Theo, who was, for his part, doing his best to be enthusiastic about everything presented to him. Perched as he was on a tiny gilt ballroom chair, the cynosure of all eyes as a prospective bridegroom, Theo was having enough of a hard time on his own.

After a polite demurral, Lady Louisa was persuaded to display her talents. The harp, a huge, gilt thing taller than the lady who proposed to play it, was dragged from its cover in the music room by two footmen, and the heir's wife, greatly increasing again, was persuaded by her fond husband to accompany Louisa on the pianoforte. A promising youth was pressed to turn the pages for her, and so the little ensemble began to warble forth a selection of English country ballads. This, it was understood, was to allow the prince to view her accomplishments.

Johannes had an ear for music, and a keen appreciation for the better composers. Lady Louisa's voice was correct but lacked passion, he thought, and Lady Seabright's playing too full of accidentals. Each offended his soul, although he was quick to join in the enthusiastic and uncritical applause at the end of each selection.

He was beginning to wonder how he could slip unnoticed from the room, and was scouting his exits when his eye fell upon Colonel Rodney, seated beside Theo.

The prince listened politely. Like his cousin, he had an ear for music, and Johannes could see each wince when an accidental was struck. He was as bored as Johannes.

But Colonel Rodney leaned forward, his lips slightly parted, his eyes wide, a flush in his cheeks. Following the line of the colonel's vision, Johannes saw Lady Louisa plucking the strings of her harp, singing a sad ballad about lost and obstructed love as she looked directly back at the colonel. The glitter in her eyes, the splash of rose in her pale cheeks—

They're in love! The young soldier and the heiress are in love, by Jove! Johannes thought. It was an interesting thought. Not that he had the least sympathy for either one of the thwarted pair, of course. Since his nature was entirely alien to the tender emotions, no one could have expected him to feel the least compassion. Rather, he thought that Rodney was a great fool to allow the object of his passions to be swallowed up by another man, especially when it was so obvious that Theo was, at best, only mildly attached to Lady Louisa.

He leaned back in his chair, his lids hooding his eyes. A faint smile played across his face. Little-known facts about well-known people were the bits of information he found most useful.

One by one, as the evening progressed, some of the older and younger men began to quietly exit the room, in search of diversion in either the billiard room or the card table, where whist was played for silver stakes. Like a hunting dog scenting its prey, Johannes sensed the opportunity for winning in the air, and very soon slipped out of his own seat and made his way down the long, long hallways in search of prey.

The duchess was reading a book of the sermons of Sydney Smith while her maid brushed her hair when the duke came into her boudoir. "That will be all, thank you, Adams," she said to her abigail, understanding that her spouse wanted a private conversation.

As soon as the maid departed the room, the duchess settled back in her chair and watched as her husband prowled the room, restlessly examining her collection of Sevres figurines. Long habit had inured her to his customs, and she waited patiently for him to formulate his thoughts.

"I say," he remarked at last, "this prince fella travels pretty simply, don't you think? Just his groom and his valet and this cousin. No entourage, none of the ceremony due a man in his position."

"He is not as conscious of his rank as one might think. When we had the Regent to stay, you will recall—"

"Please. I'd rather not think of it at all, Honoria," the duke sighed. "Every time I look at the South Lawn, I feel a most depressing sense of helplessness. A man who wasn't a duke would be angry, I think."

"Peregrine, my dear, do you have doubts about the prince?"

The duke looked gratefully at his wife. "There is a part of me that does not like the idea of dear Louisa leaving us to live in another country."

The duchess closed her book of sermons. "I quite understand. When I see The Family gathered, I feel quite mournful, when I think of Louisa absent from the family circle. One cannot help but feel—but never mind, my dear. Louisa knows what is due The Family."

"I perfectly understand, Honoria. Still, if the prince means to come up to snuff this week, and Louisa is willing to accept him, I suppose we will have to allow it."

"Louisa has been acting rather strangely of late," the duchess mused. "In one of lesser rank, it would almost seem as if she were in love."

"Love?" the duke almost exclaimed. Love, it was understood, was a rather vulgar emotion, experienced by the lower classes, but too raw, too unrefined for the daughter of a duke. "Good Lord, ma'm!"

"Exactly so," the duchess said gloomily.

"I mean, the prince is a fine fellow, but he ain't what I would call some sort of a Romeo, what?"

"Louisa has always been carefully chaperoned. There can be no question that they have been left alone together. That would never do."

"You don't suppose she's in love with someone else, do you?" the duke demanded.

"Not since she developed a crush on the second footman when she was twelve. Louisa knows what is expected of her."

"Exactly so. Well, perhaps it's just the excitement. Whatever, we shall expect the prince to address us on the subject of marriage this week."

"What if he doesn't?" the duchess asked, suddenly struck by a cold thought. "Remember the Duke of Devonshire. Sally Althorp thought he would come up to snuff for Georgina, too, and he didn't. Hunted them out of house and home, too.

"But I am sure that the prince knows exactly what is expected of him," the duchess continued. "His understanding seems quite superior to Devonshire's. Randolph says he is a complete gentleman."

"Fine fellow, Randolph. Always liked him. Always liked Cousin Robert, too. Takes after his father. Takes The Family seriously, knows his duty. When this is all out of the way, I should see about getting him a position in the Foreign Office. No telling where a fella could go with the right sponsorship behind him, what?" The duke glanced at his spouse. "You look pensive, my dear."

The duchess shook her head, then placed her night cap firmly over her hair, tying it beneath her chin. Her eyes met her husband's in the mirror. "I was only thinking," she said slowly, "how nice it would be if only Randolph were better situated in the world. He is such a *distant* cousin that there can be no question of consanguinity, and he is, after all, English, and not likely to sweep Louisa off to another country, full of foreign persons, but would keep her right here in England."

"Second thoughts?" the duke asked.

"Perhaps," the duchess replied. She squared her shoulders. "If Louisa is indeed in love with Prince Theodoric, there can be no question of standing in the way of the match."

"And if not?"

"Then I am not sure what to think. Certainly, it would be a nine days' talk in town, if the prince failed to come up to scratch. I would despise any breath of scandal."

"As would I." The duke rose. "Well, we'll see what we shall see. Well, my dear, I am glad we had this little talk." He bent and kissed her cheek. "We shall see what happens. Miss Ingersoll arrives tomorrow."

The duchess smiled. "Dear Ann! She can always be counted upon to enliven things! Good night, my love."

8

The shooting party departed quite early in the morning, long before the rest were served their morning chocolate in bed. The duke, the prince, Lord Seabright, Colonel Rodney, and the cousins set out in fine and noisy form promptly at six.

Their departure awakened Johannes from a deep sleep, and he sighed. So little time, so much to plot, he thought. A hunting accident, while convenient, would have had far too many witnesses. He sighed, punched up his pillow, and fell back into a deep sleep, dreaming of scheming ways to turn his newfound knowledge about Colonel Rodney and Lady Louisa to his own account.

Nevertheless, it is the early bird that catches the worm, and he was prompt in his appearance in the breakfast room at the stroke of nine, only to find himself the only occupant.

He availed himself of heaping helpings of eggs,

cold beef, ham, kidneys, and muffins and seated himself at the long table with the *Morning Post,* amusing himself with the Court Circular and Town Tid-Bits. He was just about to have his second cup of coffee when he heard the clatter of a carriage coming up the long, long drive, and a quarter-hour later, had the pleasure of seeing Miss Ingersoll stride into the room, still in her driving attire. She was looking very becoming, in a deep wine-colored pelisse of threaded cord, trimmed in velvet ruchings. A gray toque *à la russe* was perched on her dark curls, and her feet were shod in kid half boots. The cold air had flushed her complexion and her eyes were shining with excitement. It was clear that she had driven her phaeton and team up from town.

"What a ride we had!" she exclaimed, clearly in fine form. "It's a fine morning, and the road was clear all the way from Hammersmith!"

She greeted Johannes. "Forgive me for appearing in all my dirt, but it would appear that no one else is awake who is not out in the field shooting grouse or brakes or whatever it is they do!

"I am famished, so I thought I would eat breakfast before everyone else rises!" So saying, she helped herself at the sideboard and sat down to eat, displaying a good appetite. "Why are you not out with the rest, Count von Hazloe?"

"I have no taste for blood sports," Johannes replied. "But I am so very glad *you* are here, Miss Ingersoll."

Ann looked up at him, her eyebrows raising in a questioning look.

"Frankly, I am dying for intelligent conversation and a pleasant companion," he admitted, giving her his most devastating smile.

"Thank you, I think," Ann laughed. To his profound gratitude, she rang for the footman and instructed him to build up the fire in the grate. Like all the fires in the castle, it was not a large one. As soon as the footman had poured more coal into the grate, and stoked the flame into a cheerful blaze, warming up the room considerably, he departed, leaving the count and Miss Ingersoll to their breakfast.

"Now it is my turn to be grateful," he said. "Miss Ingersoll, do all the English all keep their houses so very cold?" His expression was so doleful that Ann had to laugh.

"I am afraid that the Coldstones live up to their name," she confessed. "They do not feel the chill, you know, who are brought up in these great old stately homes." She spread butter on a piece of muffin and bit into it, chewing thoughtfully. "Surely in Batavia, you must live in such a place yourself?"

"Oh, no, my apartments are always kept quite warm, in the palace. My side of the family is more delicate than my cousin's. We dread the cold, you know. Rather like your Mary Stuart. Wasn't it she who complained so bitterly of the cold at Hardwick?"

"You know your history, at least your English history," Ann admitted.

Johannes smiled complacently. "Oh, I know a great deal. My mother, while a misunderstood woman in many ways, was a bluestocking in her time. She left me with a great admiration for females of superior understanding, such as yourself."

If flattery were an arrow, Ann would have been shot straight through. She preened visibly under this compliment. "It is so rare that one finds a man who understands these things," she said. "Most men, and I must include your cousin in this lot, seem to think that women are intellectually inferior to them. Even the most *stupid* of them," she added darkly.

"A sad fact," Johannes agreed. He looked soulful. "A superior mind, such as your own, Miss Ingersoll, should perceive that—but I say too much! Forgive my indiscretion!"

"Perceive what?" Ann asked, genuinely curious.

"I cannot say! Forgive me, I was about to be too frank! Let us change the subject!"

Ann took the bait, just as he thought she would. "Come now, Count von Hazloe, you were about to tell me something, then you withdrew! That will not do at all. What were you about to say?"

"I cannot say! No, I cannot. Do not make me! It was an indiscretion!"

But Ann continued to work on him, and at last, he was forced, with a great show of reluctance, to give in. "I only tell you this because I know I can trust your great discretion," he said, leaning toward Ann. "But you are Lady Louisa's bosom bow! Surely you must be privy to all her most intimate secrets!"

"Well, I—" Warning signals flashed across Ann's mind, but she misread them entirely. "What has happened?"

Johannes looked suitably distressed. "Oh, nothing.

That is, nothing that should matter! It was only that I could not help but notice that Colonel Rodney and Lady Louisa—"

"Good Lord," Ann said. She laid her fork down. Her eyes searched his expression. "Whatever do you mean?" she asked cautiously.

"Dear Miss Ingersoll, believe me, I am on your side! It wrung my heart to see the look that passed between the two of them last night." Seeing Ann's expression, Johannes pressed on, describing what he had seen, and embroidering, just a little, upon it.

"I am a perceptive man, Miss Ingersoll; I see things where others might not. My heart was wrung, wrung, I tell you, by the expression on poor Lady Louisa's face as she sang that sad, sad ballad, sitting at her harp. *C'est triste, ca*! Then, to see the expression on Colonel Rodney's face, that brave soldier, to be so denied of his heart's desire . . . "

"Very touching, Count, but hardly, I think, the sign of a great romance!" Ann managed to say dryly. The fools, the pair of them, she thought! If it weren't for her, there was no telling what they might get into.

Flattery might get Johannes everywhere, under normal circumstances, but Miss Ingersoll was more cautious than he had anticipated. "I'm sure you were mistaken," she murmured.

Johannes leaned forward. "Miss Ingersoll, I am on your side. My cousin is an admirable man in many ways, but I do not think he would make suitable husband for your friend, the lovely Lady Louisa." The *lovely Lady Louisa* had such a musical ring to it, he was tempted to repeat it, but decided, after a look at

Ann, that it was best to stick to the subject at hand. "No one knows my cousin as well as I, Miss Ingersoll," he confided. "He is arrogant, proud, and headstrong!"

Seeing that he had her interest, he pursued his point. "The prince is not the man for Louisa. They would never be happy. Think of her, alone in a foreign country with only me for company. Believe me, the ladies of Batavia will be furious with the prince for marrying a foreigner! She will pine away in my country. It's so sunny and warm there!" Johannes's hand stole out and covered Ann's. "Miss Ingersoll, if there is any way to get the colonel, such a good man," he added insincerely, since he disliked Randolph Rodney almost as much as he did his cousin, "and Lady Louisa together, then certainly I am on your side."

"I don't know what to say," Ann murmured.

"Think it over, please. And remember that you have a friend in Johannes, Count von Hazloe."

Before he could pursue the conversation further, they were interrupted by the arrival of a pair of Coldstone cousins intent upon their breakfast, and their tête-à-tête was at an end.

But Johannes believed he had the confirmation of his suspicions that he needed, and he bided his time, thinking about how he could turn this to his advantage. Unfortunately, thinking was so exhausting that he soon had to retire to the library, where he was able to lie down for a while on the sofa, safe, for the moment, from Coldstones.

Just as he was drifting into a pleasant postprandial nap, his repose was rudely interrupted by the unexpected appearance of the Lords Gerald and Charles, the Seabrights' two lively offspring, followed in hot pursuit by four or five of their young cousins, who had escaped the charge of their various nannies, and were playing at wild Indians. They summarily declared Johannes their prisoner. The result was that the hapless count was hog-tied with the curtain pulls and forgotten, his cries for help going unheeded in the empty corridors until an underhouse parlor maid, going about her dusting, discovered him in a most undignified position as he rolled on the floor attempting to free himself.

Unfortunately, she mistook him for the family ghost, the Restoration beauty Arabella Coldstone known as the Green Lady, whose headless specter roamed that area of the castle. She caused such a ruckus with her terrified screams that the butler and several footmen came running to her assistance.

The result was a rumor that quickly spread through the servants' hall that Count von Hazloe was the sort of man who attempted to take liberties with the maids. This did not increase his popularity with the staff, who had already marked him down as a poor tipper. A hundred subtle ways were found to make his stay even less comfortable.

When, inevitably, the rumor reached the ears of his hostess, the duchess pursed her lips, shook her head, and sighed. "What a humbug! My dearest little grandsons are angels of propriety," she pronounced. "Blaming innocent children is very typical of foreigners." She commanded the butler to keep a discreet eye on Johannes from now on. "It's harder to find good help than foreign counts," she observed wisely.

Johannes, whose amoratory hook was cast for far wealthier and more socially important fish than mere housemaids, would have been humiliated had he known. Ignorance is not always bliss.

Meanwhile, Lady Louisa had awakened from her slumbers and was greeting Ann with suitable exclamations, as if they had not parted only a few days before. While Louisa sipped morning chocolate and Ann drew off her gloves and hat and freshened her toilette, they put their heads together.

"Joseph Potter and I left before dawn this morning. I left my maid to come on behind with the trunks by post chaise. She should be here this afternoon! No sense in having more than one team eating its head off in your father's stables, with so many Coldstone horses to be fed! It was a glorious ride! The day was crisp and traffic was light! We made it in five hours!"

Ann threw herself down on the bed and selected a piece of toast from the rack on Louisa's tray. "Keating was, of course, fit to be tied, since she thinks no lady should drive a phaeton at all, let alone drive one on a public road with just a groom for company, but let me tell you, Joseph is far more censorious of my behavior than even my father!"

"Well, I am glad you are here, Ann. Randolph is in agony. He's convinced this entire idea is mad, utterly mad, and that his friendship with the prince is in jeopardy. At least they're all out shooting today, so Prince Theodoric can't have The Talk with Papa."

"And it is my job to tell you both to be more discreet. I was having breakfast this morning when the count informed me that he had seen you and Randolph exchanging lovelorn looks across the room last night. He means to adapt himself to whatever plans we make."

Ann bit into her toast. "Cold. Give me some of that strawberry jam, that's a love," she said, reaching for the spoon.

"What? The count saw us? But we've been so discreet!" Louisa exclaimed.

"No stolen moments behind the boxwood maze? No clandestine meetings in the Picture Gallery? What is wrong with you two?" Ann spread a generous amount of jam on her toast and bit into it, rolling over among Louisa's silk pillows.

"When you know that you are going to be together forever and ever, then you don't need stolen moments. We're Coldstones." Louisa fluffed up her hair.

"I wouldn't be too certain that this is going to work," Ann said thoughtfully, licking jam from her fingers. "Perhaps you ought to think about stealing some moments, somewhere."

But Louisa, whose experience of the world was limited, and who had nearly always been so extremely *good*, remained sanguine. "Of course it will work. And Papa will be furious with the prince, and that will be that."

"Whatever you say, I'm sure I wouldn't know.

Besides, the prince might just win the race. An odious thought, that."

"It doesn't signify. Whatever happens, Papa will be furious. Five hundred pounds! He was miffed last night because Uncle Louis and Cousin Rupert sat down to play whist at half crown points with the count!"

"Well, he will be furious with me, too!"

"Oh, but he doesn't *stay* mad at you," Louisa said practically. "He and Mama love you far too much for that." She sipped her chocolate, regarding Ann over the rim of the cup.

"Be that as it may," Ann said. She rose from the bed and looked out the window. "Louisa, I think it looks like snow!"

"You know, it looks like it's clouding over," Theo said to Randolph.

The colonel looked up at the sky, where ragged gray clouds were moving slowly from the west. "It looks like it may snow."

"Yes, I think so," Theo said, not looking at his friend. "Snow we shall have."

He rubbed his hands together, trying to work the cold out of his blood. They were a little apart from the rest of the shooting party, walking along the hedgerows and the brown stubbled fields toward the castle. It had been a successful hunt. The beaters had beaten and the valets had loaded and handed off the guns, a score of partridges had been bagged, and voluminous shot and powder had been expended, making a great deal of noise. A handsome lunch had been unpacked from picnic hampers and scotch whiskey had been consumed to warm the bones. Best, the men had gotten away from all but the most sporting of the women and done manly things, a welcome relief from the social world, where women ran the show and made the rules. "After all, duke or laborer, a man's get to hunt, what?" the duke said, neatly summing it all up for all concerned.

The partridges would be hung, and after being suitably aged for a week or so, served for dinner.

"It reminds me of the old days, you know, when we were running and fighting in the hills," Theo recalled, "Those clouds. The way we could never have a fire, for fear the smoke could betray us to the French."

A smile flickered over Randolph's features. "I remember that. By God, we were alive, then, weren't we?"

"Cold, wet, hungry, and miserable, but alive. All of this, this luxury, seems so different after all of that. We grew to know each other as well as we knew ourselves."

"True enough."

"So, when I sense something is bothering you— and I've had that sense for the past fortnight—I wait to see what you will say. And you say nothing, Randolph. What is it? Money? A female? Come, my friend, there's nothing you can't tell me. Perhaps I can help you."

"Your Highness—Theo—" Randolph said suddenly, stopping in his tracks. "Damn, man! Why do you make this all so hard?"

Theo brought up short, peering at Randolph's anguished features. "This is serious, isn't it?" he asked.

"More than you have any idea," Randolph replied uneasily. "I am your friend, Theo and I have done you the worst thing anyone could do to a friend!"

Theo frowned. "What do you mean? Out with it man! Good God, it wasn't you who took a shot at me in the park, was it?"

It was Randolph's turn to be startled. "Shot at you? In the park? What are you talking about? What happened?"

Theo looked at him closely. He knew Randolph well enough to know that the colonel was genuinely shocked. It was then that he understood how little trust he had placed in anyone, even his closest friends, since he had taken the throne. "Well," Theo said calmly, "when I was riding with Miss Ingersoll in the park that day, you recall, someone took a shot at me. At the time, I thought it was an accident, but since then, I have wondered—"

"Why didn't you tell me this before? Why didn't you tell someone? Why didn't Ann tell me about it?"

"Because I asked her not to. I think that I persuaded her that it was an accident, someone playing with a gun, but a ball grazed my cheek. Caused a little scratch, but nothing serious. Fortunately, there was no great harm done, aside from upsetting those fine grays of hers, and I was able to pass the incident off as a mere nothing to my people when I returned to the residence."

"Do you think your enemies are after you again? I

thought that matter was all settled, in Batavia, after the Restoration," Randolph said, "when Parliament was reconvened."

"Evidently not. I thought they had all gone into exile with the Bonaparte collaborators. But I must face the fact that there is a traitor among those I should trust, someone who has been corrupted by the, shall I say, disloyal opposition. Someone who would like to see me harmed on English soil. It would certainly put a period to the trade agreements I have worked so hard negotiate with the English, and would mean that we would have no choice but to deal with the French wine-growing interests. In effect, to remove me would be to quash any hope Batavia could have for an independent economy."

"I had thought—I had hoped—that when you were restored to the throne, they would have seen the folly of continuing to oppose the will of the people," Randolph said. "We knew, we suspected that there were elements who didn't wish you well, but—"

"I had hoped that they would work within Parliament for peaceful change," Theo said. "I had hoped with the reestablishment of suffrage and the vote that people would see that it can no longer be government by a handful of the wealthy and powerful, but by all."

"Johannes is in this, isn't he?"

Theo laughed and clapped his friend on the back. "Whenever you find a scheme against me, you find Johannes there! Why did you think I brought him with me? Not because I like his company, but to keep an eye on the fool! No, Randolph, he is being used by others more powerful than he, more cunning. But I have a feeling that only through him will I prove who the traitors are. We have our suspicions at home, you know." He pronounced two names Randolph recognized; both high-born Batavians, both men who had profited under the reign of the Bonaparte cousin. "But they are being watched closely, and their communications intercepted. Thank God there are those I know I can trust!"

Randolph shuddered. "Good Lord, Theo, I don't envy you," he said. "If I had been you, I would have thrown it all over long ago."

"I can't," Theo said simply. "This is my duty."

"Then what are we to do? You know I cannot allow you to go through this alone. A message to the Foreign Office would—"

"No, no! Nothing for now; I prefer to handle this myself. I think as long as we are at Coldstone, I am safe; they prefer public places, rather than enclosed and private lands, I think. Now, they failed once, and no doubt they will try again, but they do not know that I am on my guard, and ready for an unknown–or known—assassin." Theo looked at his friend. "I've been through worse, as well you know." He grinned a singularly diabolical grin, the ghost of the young soldier he had once been. "I'll survive this! Now, enough! Tell me what has you so hipped, Colonel Rodney!"

Randolph sighed, pushing a hand over his fair hair. "How can I, after what you have told me?" he asked. "Whatever I would say would add to your burdens."

"Or it might relieve them," the prince said cheerfully. "Come on, out with it! We've been friends a fair piece, you know. Whatever it is, it can't be as bad as the night the French has us pinned down in that farmhouse in the valley."

"I feel much as I did then! Surrounded on all sides!" the Colonel recalled with a shudder.

"And yet, we came out of that one aright, and lost only one man, more was the miracle!"

"True. Oh, Lord, Theo, if this were as simple as a battle! Any time women are concerned in the matter, you know that it will become too complicated! But I thought, I really did think, if I could not marry her, then you would make her happy. I had not the faintest idea that she returned my feelings—damn! Why is it so hard to talk about—love?"

"Because we're a pair of hardened old soldiers!" Theo retorted. He put a hand on Randolph's shoulder. "Tell it straight, old man! You are in love with Lady Louisa!"

"Yes!" Randolph cried, in agony.

To his great surprise, Theo started to laugh. It was a rich, deep chuckle that started somewhere deep in his chest and burst through his lips in a series of shouts.

"Well, I don't think there's anything to be amused about," Randolph retorted, stung. "We're talking about a lady here!"

"Yes, yes we are! A fine lady, a marvelous woman, and a great beauty! Yes, she is a great beauty, if you like pink and white blonds! She is everything that is attractive, and I congratulate you!"

"Now, see here, Prince! You're talking about the

woman I love here! Your fiancée!" Randolph said heatedly.

"No, not yet my fiancée, thank God! Oh, yes, yes, Randolph! The Lady Louisa is in every way a most admirable female, but I have no more wish to marry her than to fly to the moon!"

"Are you trying to say she's not good enough for you?" Randolph inquired testily. "She's a Coldstone, sir!"

"Oh, don't be such a blockhead, Colonel! Of course she's good enough for me! In fact, she might be too good for me! Yes, indeed, she is!"

"This might be amusing to you, sir," Randolph said with awful formality, "but for me, it is a matter of deadly seriousness."

His words only caused Theo to laugh the harder. "No, no, no! Colonel, forgive me, I am not laughing at you or Lady Louisa! No, I am happy for you both! Allow me to wish you well! I think she will make you an excellent wife! She is everything that is good and amiable and beautiful, but she and I—dammit, man can't you see that we would never suit? Within six months, we'd both be going our separate ways, or worse! I have been wondering since I arrived here how I could extricate myself from this situation! I know that she and I are no more suited than chalk and cheese."

"Oil and water," Colonel Rodney corrected him. "Do you mean to say that you don't want to marry Louisa?"

"No more than she wants to marry me, which I think is to say not at all!" He put out his hand. "Allow me to congratulate you! Felicitations! Allow me to stand godfather to your first child!" His laughter slowly faded, but his smile remained as he gazed fondly at his friend.

"But, Theo, sir, Your Highness—"

"No buts. If you and Lady Louisa are settled, then no one could be happier than I! Lord, man, I've no wish to be Benedick! Plenty of bachelor days left for me! Marry I must, but not for some time, I hope!"

Colonel Rodney's sigh was audible. The two men walked along the hedgerow for some time in silence, each one occupied with his own thoughts. Gradually, Randolph began to snicker; the snicker rose to a chuckle, the chuckle to a guffaw, and soon he was laughing as heartily as the prince.

"Oh, my foolish friend, I am thankful you spoke when you did! You might have allowed us both to make a tragic mistake!" Theo exclaimed.

"There is still a major obstacle to overcome," Randolph said, suddenly serious again. "The duke and duchess would never hear of it. Have their daughter marry a half-pay officer with sinister connections in intelligence? Espionage, my friend, is not what people like my cousins find a respectable profession. And how would I support Louisa? What could she expect?" He grimaced. "She thinks we can live in a cottage, that we should elope! But I think too much of her for such an escapade! She knows nothing about the way life is lived in the real world, you know. She has been raised in such a sheltered life!"

"I think she will adapt herself to whatever life brings her. She may be naive, but she is not without resources, you know. One thing about people like the duke and duchess, they bring up their children to face any situation that might be presented to them, you know! Why, I daresay that if you were to elope and live in a cottage, it would not be long 'ere Lady Louisa was conversant with all aspects of domestic management! Sweeping floors, dressing a joint, why I daresay none of these things would dismay her for long!"

"No, I suppose you are right, but it still doesn't remove the objections of the duke and duchess!"

"How do you know they would object? Have you asked?"

"How can I when they have their hearts set on Louisa marrying a prince—namely yourself?" Randolph asked despondently. "If you had a daughter, who would you want her to marry? A man like me or a man like you?"

"I would embrace the modern notion that she should marry a man with whom she can be happy, of course. Come now, we no longer live in the Dark Ages! The duke and duchess love their daughter, they are sincerely fond of you, and if something were found objectionable about me, and you pressed your suit, well!"

"You sound like Ann, Miss Ingersoll, I mean! You would believe the idea Louisa cooked up and she has agreed to!" Carefully, Randolph laid the racing plot bare.

The prince's reaction was interesting. As he listened, he frowned. Then he swore beneath his breath, then he swore aloud and turned the air blue, then he shook his head, scowling. "That woman is a vixen, Randolph! I knew the minute I laid eyes on her that she was trouble! Who does she think she's fooling? Who does she think I am? Some bumpkin who just fell off the grape wagon?"

"It was a sort of girlish fancy, cooked up between the pair of them. If you blame one, you may as well blame the other, but I know that they meant well!" Randolph apologized.

"Five hundred pounds! She wagered five hundred pounds that her grays could beat my chestnuts, and I accepted! And then she planned to make a fool out of me! Trouble! That woman is trouble, and she needs to be taught a lesson!"

"Now, Theo, when you calm down, you'll think better of it all," Randolph cautioned him. "She only meant to help us, don't you see?"

"Yes, but she meant to do it at my expense! I am a crown prince, Randolph! No mere chit of a girl is going to make a fool out of me!"

"Come on, Theo, allow it to rest! A schoolgirl prank, although an ill-advised one, is no reason to rant and rage! You have other, more important things to worry about than Ann Ingersoll!"

"A spoiled heiress! Lord, I pity her father! I pity that poor dry stick of a man to whom she has attached herself! She will no doubt lead Mr. Briggs a merry chase, but she will not, cannot top me! No! She will not make a fool out of me!" Theo said, fire sparking in his eyes.

"But, Theo, you are not—"

"No, I suppose I am acting from anger, and that is

always a very bad thing," Theo mused, forcing himself to calm down. "After all, the ladies, however crackbrained their scheme, were acting in what they believe to be the best interests of both you and Lady Louisa. Still, I think Miss Ingersoll needs to learn something about a woman's place in the world!"

"Theo, when you get like this, I tremble," Randolph said cautiously.

"No, no need! I think all can be arranged most discreetly. Perhaps it would be better if Lady Louisa were kept in the dark about my plan. I had meant to allow Miss Ingersoll to win the race, but now, I think not. And," he added with a grin, "I think the stakes will be raised!"

9

It was not until the company sat down to dinner that night that Theo caught his first glimpse of Ann. It was, of course, partially obscured by the epergne, but he was able to observe that she was very much in looks. For some reason, this annoyed Theo, who felt, unreasonably, that she ought to have the grace to look like a guilty coconspirator, rather than an elegant female very much at her ease among these superior Coldstones. That he was unaccountably annoyed irritated him even more, and he was able to lay his unbecoming emotions solidly upon her doorstep. How dare she think that a mere female could best a man like Prince Theodoric of Batavia?

Ann was looking her best in a celestial blue dinner dress with a silver net crêpe overslip. Her hair was dressed high on her head and a profusion of dark curls fell around her cheeks. Teardrop sapphire and diamond earrings depended from her lobes, and her décolleté was enhanced by a lavaliere of the same gems. As she turned to address her companion on the right, she smiled, and he was rather annoyed to see that she was addressing his cousin Johannes. As he watched, their heads moved closer together, and they shared a private remark that made both of them laugh.

His wounded pride, always a besetting sin, hardened his determination to see this impertinent girl brought low. How could she even think that a mere female could best a man such as himself?

No woman had ever attempted to fool Prince Theodoric. Well, that was, strictly speaking, not totally true, he reflected darkly, there were those who had tried—and failed. It would, he thought, sipping at his wine, be a pleasure to add Miss Ingersoll to that list. She was the most infuriating woman he had ever had the misfortune to meet in his lifetime! The sad thing was, he was almost beginning to like her until Randolph's unfortunate disclosure.

Well, she would have to learn her lesson, that was all. And he was just the man to teach her. . . .

"As I was saying, Prince, when I was visiting your country in '98, I met a man named Baron Threzha, or was his name Baron Thesla?" the elderly dowager at his right was saying as she addressed her fish course with gusto. A great many dirty diamonds flashed on her fingers and wrists, and her small black eyes were hawklike. "Anyway, he knew my late husband, I believe they met in Paris in '86. My husband knew Prince Metternich. Did you know the Duchesse de Dino, Prince Theodoric? She was a most interesting woman. Always had a pack of little dogs trailing around her, or was that Princess Esterhazy? At any rate, it was one of those foreign peeresses, don't you know. She might have been Hungarian. Do you have any Hungarians in your family line? I met a Hungarian archduke in Scotland once. At least he said he was an archduke. Might have been a Russian. I don't recall ever having met any von Hazloes or und Gottfreunds before. In my day, one was either English or one wasn't and that was that."

He was dragged inexorably back into her reminiscences of people and places of a generation before his time, most of whom were either unknown to him or, he suspected, ghosts of her senile memories. With a great effort, he dragged his attention away from Miss Ingersoll at the other end of the table, and whatever Johannes was saying to make her laugh in such a way, and fastened it upon the hawk-eyed matron.

"Are the von Hazloes related to Charlemagne, young man?" she asked. "The Coldstone-Blights can trace themselves to him, you know. Is that a real title or a Papal title? What was your mother's maiden name? Are your family members of the Holy Roman Empire? Are you related to the Thrum und Taxis? I met a Prince Thrum und Taxis once in London. Or was it Almack's during the Peace Celebrations? No, that was Prince Haakon of Denmark. He married a daughter of the Elektor of Hesse. Or do I mean the Landgrave of Hesse? Or was that Graf von—now what was his name? He had a mustache. . . ."

With an inward sigh, Prince Theo resigned himself to explaining the convoluted history of titled

Continental families and his own ancestry for the dowager's edification, if not her complete satisfaction. That last, he began to feel, after her thirtieth question, was beyond the instrumentality of any mortal.

He felt a profound sense of relief when the game course arrived and he was able to turn the tables and speak to Lady Seabright on his other side.

"Do you hunt, Prince Theodoric?" was her first question. Lord and Lady Seabright were known to be hunting mad, to the extent that Lady Seabright hilltopped the pack right up to the moment of her last confinement and might have delivered at the point rather than miss the kill, had not clearer heads prevailed. "What is the hunting like in Batavia?"

Theo smiled. "Humbug country," he replied.

Her conversation might have been limited to the subject of fox hunting, but he found it far easier to discuss the breeding of Irish hunters than people. And was able to relax slightly and allow her steady stream of chatter about the lack of good hunting in the Coldstone environs flow while he concentrated his thoughts on being irritated by Miss Ingersoll.

Meanwhile on the other side of the epergne, "I'm so glad we're dining *en famille,* so that precedent is set aside," Johannes was confiding to Ann. "Otherwise, I might not have had the pleasure of dining with you." He proceeded, putting himself in the best possible light, to recount the story of his capture by Lords Gerald and Charles, and his subsequent release. "Children and dogs, Miss Ingersoll must forever be separate from my sphere. I wonder why it should be that they both dislike me so much, when one is forever as open as the sun?"

Ann laughed, shaking her head. "I fear that the duke and duchess are indulgent to a sad degree with their grandchildren. I think it is always that way with those who are very strict with their own offspring. But it was very bad of them to pretend you were a settler and tie you up like that."

Johannes sighed. "It is but one more reason why I hope my cousin declares himself to the duke very soon! Believe me, there is nothing here that can keep me from yearning for the pleasures of London! The country always makes me feel so *dépaysé*, don't you know. It is so—so *bucolic*!" He made a droll face. "I am a man of the Metropolis, don't you know; I have no comprehension for this very English love of the country!"

Ann took pity on him; his expression was so woeful, his story so outrageous that she surrendered to impulse. What could it possibly hurt, she wondered. "You may be back in town soon, Count. I have a, oh, a feeling, that Prince Theodoric will be leaving soon."

"Re-ally," Johannes said, immediately intrigued. "Dear, dear Miss Ingersoll, I beg of you, consider me your willing servant in any scheme, that is to say, any plan you might have that will return me to London as soon as possible! Call it a humanitarian gesture! Please, I would do anything to be warm and comfortable again!"

At that moment, the footmen began to remove the game course, and the tables were turned. Ann smiled,

"Later!" she promised, and turned politely toward her other neighbor, leaving Johannes to stare at a cooling slice of tough veal placed before him.

After dinner, it was decided that the young people would dance, and accordingly, the rugs were rolled away in the music room. Lady Seabright was pressed into service on the pianoforte and Cousin Floyd Coldstone lent his talents on the fiddle. Those who did not participate sat around the edges of the room, fanning themselves and declaring how warm it was while they kept an eagle's eye on the dancers, watching for any signs of impropriety. The Coldstones, to a cadet branch, did not approve of impropriety. Like the sails of a ship under full sail, the duchess's plumes nodded majestically as she rounded up the dancers, sorting them into partners and sets.

The prince bowed to Lady Louisa and opened the dancing with her, leading her in a slow waltz. Two or three of the younger people began to join them, but the evening began slowly, since so many of those present did not know this new dance just then being accepted in London.

The duchess, who was nothing if not a proficient hostess, gave the command to her daughter-in-law to play some country dances that they all knew.

"Will you make up a set in the Sir Roger de Coverly?" she told, not asked the prince, quite firmly moving him into the middle of the floor. "Ah, dear Ann! I know you can be trusted to help break the ice! Dance, my dear, with Prince Theodoric. You know all the steps."

Not by as much as a twitch of his eyebrow did Theo betray his feelings as he was sorted into a set with Miss Ingersoll and a pair of cousins. To look at him, one would never know what boiled beneath that polite surface. His diplomatic training stood him in good stead.

Miss Ingersoll, oblivious to the fate the prince had planned for her, rose to the occasion. "Well, Your Highness, I see we find ourselves partners again. Do you know our English country dances, sir?"

"I believe so, Miss Ingersoll," he replied gravely, and spun her through a few practice movements that made her head spin.

"I see that you do," Ann murmured when she recovered her balance. "Well!"

"Indeed!" The prince smiled a trifle grimly. "When did you arrive, Miss Ingersoll?"

"Oh, my groom and I left London quite early this morning! My grays are in prime shape for a go. And your chestnuts?"

"Ready to overtake your grays," he replied seriously.

They turned, bowed, and parted, coming back together again. "Ah! You think you can beat me?" she asked quizzically.

"I know I can best you in any equestrian competition," Theo assured her loftily. He bowed, they separated and faced the other couple, coming together to skip down the line, where they took their places at the end, clapping in time to the music as the other couples made the skip.

Reels were formed again, and several figures danced before they came together again. "So, you can best me in any equestrian competition," Ann repeated, smiling, but dubious.

"The male of the species, Miss Ingersoll, is by his very nature, superior to the female."

"What a humbug you are, Prince!" Ann replied gaily. "We poor females only allow you great goobies to think so!"

"Great goobies? *Goobies*?" the prince exclaimed, but Miss Ingersoll had danced away.

"No, Your Highness, my name is Georgina," said the timid young lady who was suddenly standing up with him. "Georgy Coldstone!"

"Oh yes, quite," the prince replied vacantly. he forced himself to smile. "Now see here, Miss Ingersoll, I am not a gooby, whatever that may be," he said sternly when they were face to face once again.

"I didn't say that you were, Your Highness, only that men *in general* tend to be great goobies," Ann said sweetly.

They turned, bowed, and parted. The prince was left to digest this for several measures before they were brought face to face again.

"At least men are not flibbertigibbets!" he replied. "Flirting, skirting heart-renders who cajole and manage! What do you say to that?"

"That it is men who have put us in this position. You say it is for our own benefit, that we are the inferior sex, but in reality, it is so that we are forced to bend, by law and by custom, to your will! Nay, your whim!"

"Well, perhaps you would like to up the stakes on our little wager!"

"Perhaps I might!"

"Consider this, then; the loser must publicly declare that the winner's sex is superior in every fashion!"

"Agreed!"

They parted again, and when they came together, neither one of them had anything more to say. They glared at each other sullenly, and bowed formally when the dance was over, separating without comment.

Johannes, who had very properly been dancing with the duchess, had kept a weather eye on events. He was agog with curiosity as to what had been said, and wasted no time in engaging Miss Ingersoll for a promenade.

"From the stormy look in those lovely eyes, I would guess that my royal cousin has managed to put up your back. On behalf of the von Hazloes, I apologize!"

"Your cousin is odious," Ann said firmly. "Overbearing, arrogant, and conceited!"

"Tell me that which I do not know!" Johannes said sympathetically.

"Well, perhaps I should tell you. After all, you could be of help to me, to us, rather!" Ann said.

"I have informed you that I am at your feet, Miss Ingersoll; whatever I can do, I would do it willingly!"

"Then I will tell you. But you must give me your word, your word of honor as a gentleman that no matter what, you will not breathe a word to anyone else!"

"Oh, I can give you my word of honor as a gentle-

man," Johannes easily assured her with his most
charming smile. "Now, come sit down and tell me
everything, Miss Ingersoll."

10

That night, word of the impending race spread through the assembled company. Even after they had retired, there was much talking in the corridors and assembling in various bedrooms to discuss the forthcoming competition.

Before the evening was out, the battle lines were drawn and sides were chosen up.

The ladies, hearing that the prince had declared no mere female could ever best a man, aligned themselves on Ann's side, while the gentlemen tended to favor Theo.

"I rather like Miss Ingersoll's chances," the duchess said, looking around at the assembled Coldstone women in her boudoir. "She is a natural whip. But has anyone ever seen Prince Theodoric drive?"

Cousin Cordelia said she had seen him driving in the park, but it was hard to judge his skills by a glimpse on Rotten Row.

Lady Seabright, inveterately equine, laced her fingers over the forthcoming Seabright and pronounced that her choice would be Miss Ingersoll, all things considered. "For her hands are good, and she is quick. I don't know about the prince; he talks like a man that rushes his fences."

Everyone nodded. Lady Seabright was held to be a great judge of these things.

"Well, Ann, I think we shall be crowning you the victor!" Cousin Cordelia said. "Have a little toddy, my dear, to keep the chill away."

For the gentlemen, gathered in the smoking room, talk centered on Prince Theodoric's prowess.

"Well, here now, Your Highness, watch those hands, you'll need them tomorrow, mark my words," Lord Seabright said, putting a pillow under the prince's wrist.

"Those chestnuts looks like sixteen-mile-an-hour tits," offered Cousin Rupert Coldstone. "Great goers!"

"The lady has the stamina, but she'll fade, because, well damn, man, females just don't have the strength to go a long course," declared Uncle George Coldstone.

"That," declared the prince, "is what I am counting on." He allowed Lord Seabright to light his cigarillo, while Cousin Albert Coldstone poured him another glass of whiskey.

The men all chuckled, secure in their male superiority.

*   *   *

By morning, the entire household knew that the prince and Miss Ingersoll had agreed to race their teams, and interest ran high. Some declared that the prince would win easily; others, who knew Miss Ingersoll's skill as a whip, declared she would make the finish line well before His Highness.

"My money is on my lady," Joseph Potter said in the servant's hall.

Murdo, Theo's man, disagreed. "My prince, he is a driver! You will see!" he declared loyally. "There is no one who can handle a team like him!"

Glaring at one another, both men went out to the stables to inspect the horses and the carriages.

After a peaceful night in which she lost no sleep, Ann descended the stairs the next morning, sweeping the train of her bottle-green riding coat up over one arm. It was cut in a severe military style, with a double row of gold buttons down the snug bodice and the shoulders topped with epaulettes. She was looking very dashing, having left Keating's hands with her curls tucked up beneath a bronze-colored velvet bonnet trimmed with feathers that curled around her cheek. In her hand, she carried a pair of York tan gloves, and on her feet she wore neat brown leather half boots. She was feeling quite confident of herself and her grays, having received word from Joseph Potter that all was in shape to go.

She found the prince devouring a hearty breakfast, and in a jovial mood, surrounded as he was by his male supporters. It was not long before Ann was joined by the ladies, and there was a great deal of good-natured banter back and forth; this was the most exciting event that had been presented for the guests' entertainment so far.

"Not," Cousin Cordelia murmured to Cousin Rupert, "that *that* says a great deal."

"I don't suppose you would like to wager on the outcome?" General Coldstone asked his brother the admiral. "A little something on the lady at five to one, say?"

"Brothers, brothers, *gambling*?" the duke asked in pained tones.

"Oh, I say, Binky, it's only a little money, nothing extravagant, just a few guineas," the admiral said, shuffling his feet and thrusting his hands into his pockets like the little brother he once had been.

The duke frowned. "Be that as it may, you know how I feel about wagering. Not that I am against anyone having a little enjoyment, but the whole point should be the race itself, not betting. Remember Father!"

The general and the admiral did indeed remember their profligate father, but since neither felt that a five guinea bet was the first step on the road to the sponging house, they did what they had done since time immemorial and placed their bets where their brother could not see them.

This practice was followed by others wise in the ways of the duke's prejudices, and a quietly surreptitious betting book was started in the smoking room, with a surprising number of Coldstones anxious to lay their wagers one way or the other.

Apparently not all of the Coldstones remembered Grandfather.

After breakfast that morning, the duke and the contestants retired to the library.

The duke drew down a map of his estate and mapped out the course, which would run from the Grand Drive, over the lanes through the estate gardens, and across the roads that connected the home farm to the tenants' estates to the ruins of an old priory, then back along the same course, a distance of about twenty miles.

Ann, who knew the territory well, studied the map and nodded. "The hills are the tricky part, through the Home Wood," she told the prince. "That's a lonely stretch."

The prince, who had surveyed the lay of the land while hunting the previous day, nodded as he bent to study the map.

"I've made you each a copy. When you reach the old priory ruins, you will each find a pennant, which you will bring back here. I judge the race should take no more than three or four hours. You understand that all the rules of fair play and honor apply, and you will be expected to act like gentle—like ladies and gentlemen. Like a lady and a gentleman!" He gasped for breath and mopped his forehead. The duke was not a man who enjoyed lengthy explanations. "Do you understand?"

"I do," Theo said a trifle grimly.

"I understand, " Ann said.

The prince and Miss Ingersoll glared at each other.

"Well, then, let us proceed," the duke said. "I understand that your people have prepared your teams and they are waiting outside.

"If there are no more questions, let us proceed."

There was little difference between the temperature inside and out, both being briskly frosty, but Ann glanced warily up at the skies, which were gray with full, puffy clouds. The air, she thought, was so clean out in the country, where there were none of the London chimneys and fogs to fill the air with thick, pungent city smells. By nightfall, she guessed, there would be snow. She drew the collar of her coat closer around her neck and wished she had not disregarded Keating's admonition to wear a scarf. It would be a cold ride. But, she hoped, a short one.

The prince was studying the sky, too, with the expert eye of one who has lived outdoors. A thin line appeared between his eyebrows, and he drew on his gloves, glad for the warmth of his driving coat with its many capes, and an extra pair of wool stockings inside his heavy riding boots. He adjusted his flat crowned beaver on his dark hair and set his jaw grimly, as if he were going into battle.

Which, in a way, he was, he reflected.

Several carriages were waiting at the grand portico. It was the avowed intention of many to follow the race through various vantage points around the estate, and the mood was high.

Lady Seabright, dusting off her gloves, was just finishing her inspection of the phaeton and the curricle. The two vehicles, their teams harnessed and ready, stood waiting, held by their respective grooms.

"Your grays look fatigued, Miss Ingersoll," Theo drawled, walking around her team. "You must have exhausted them coming down here yesterday."

"Whereas, my dear prince," Ann replied, running her hand across the flank of one of the chestnuts, "these horses haven't been out of their stalls in two days. They could very easily run away with you."

There were twitters in the watching crowd of Coldstones. Louisa, seated in her brother's barouche, looked anxiously at Colonel Rodney, who hovered nearby on his bay gelding and was doing his best *not* to look anxious, although it was hard for him to keep from looking at Louisa more than he should have done, had he wished to be discreet.

"Where is Johannes?" Randolph suddenly demanded. "Has anyone seen Count von Hazloe?"

No one could say that they had. Randolph's jaw set in a hard line, and he reined his horse in. "I'll catch up with you later," he promised, and rode away.

But fortunately, no one was paying any attention to the thwarted lovers. All eyes were on the show in the middle of the cobblestone courtyard, where Joseph Potter was throwing Ann up into the high seat of the phaeton, murmuring advice into her ear like a prize-fighter's manager.

Theo did not need Murdo's help to mount into his curricle, but as he wove the ribbons around his fingers, he sensed that the chestnuts were restless, feeling their enormous power through the leather reins as they moved, ready to be off. They were, he thought, too fresh.

Standing on the portico, the duchess at his side with her opera glasses primed, the duke looked at his big gold pocket watch. He held a dueling pistol up as Ann and Theo brought their teams in line on the cobbles.

"Ready?" he called?

"Ready!" Ann said with a little more confidence than she was really feeling.

"Yes!" The prince called, winding his muffler about his neck.

One of the grays whinnied, sensing the tension in the air. "Go!" The pistol discharged with a loud explosion.

The onlookers cheered.

The curricle and the phaeton both bolted at one time; with a jingling of harnesses and a sharp, echoing clatter of hooves, they were off, neck and neck down the long drive through the Italian statues and the old yew trees, clattering on the cobblestones until they reached the gates.

Ann looked neither to the right nor the left, but kept her attention focused on the ears of the right leader and the road ahead, just as Joseph Potter had taught her. The wind whistled through her earrings, stinging at her cheeks, making her eyes water, and she began to roll with the springs of the phaeton, allowing her body to follow the rhythm of the team, allowing the grays to have just a little of their head, yet holding the ribbons back just enough so that they never had their full burst. She did not want to wear them down immediately, for she knew that they would need that spirit later. Still, she was anxious to allow them to wear off that initial energy.

Outside the gates, the open, rolling fields of the estate spread out before her. She was dimly aware of the curricle nearby, the chestnuts sometimes before her, sometimes trailing her, of a cheering as they passed a vantage point where several estate carriages waited to watch them race on. As soon as they passed, the carriages moved across the pathways between the fields, looking for the next vantage point.

After a while, she pulled back a little, saving the grays, bringing them from a gallop down into a canter, pleased with the way they responded to her hands. She sat up very straight, keeping her eyes on the brown and rutted roads that twisted and turned through the stubbled fields.

About an hour later, she passed a cluster of people from the farms who stood near the barns, agog with curiosity to watch the nobs race across the estate. Ann was aware of their eyes following her, the way in which they stared and pointed. Someone was yelling, but she could not catch their words above the noise of the horses' hooves. The duke, unlike many other landowners, had not enclosed his land.

And so she pushed on, the phaeton swaying dangerously on its leather springs, suspended so high above the yellow wheels.

She was dimly aware that snow had begun to fall, large, fat flakes that she licked from her lips, grateful for the moisture; her mouth was *so* dry.

Dimly, she was aware of the Coldstone carriages perched on the top of a nearby hill. She passed them smartly, waving as she did so.

The woods loomed up ahead of her, thick and tangled. The forest primeval, she and Louisa used to call it, where the road was a narrow rutted pathway through the old trees. She slowed again, not wanting to break an axle on the ruts, or have one of her horses break a leg in a chuckhole. The snow fell, even in here, spiraling down between the skeletal branches of the trees. It was, she noticed, growing thicker, beginning to accumulate.

She looked around, and saw Theo about twenty yards behind her. He raised his whip in greeting.

She waved and turned around, feeling an odd sense of relief. And so they went into the forest, heading for the old priory ruins.

The woods seemed very still. It was as if something had reached out and swallowed her up. She glanced around again but the road had curved behind her and she could not see Theo.

It seemed like a week before she reached the clearing in the woods, where the ruins of the ancient priory had once stood. As promised, two pennants bearing the arms of Coldstone Castle had been planted there on stakes. By now, she was cold and tired, and she could feel that the grays were straining. She reached out and grasped the pennant; it released itself from the stake. Ann tucked it into her sleeve and turned the phaeton around. The snow was falling thick and fast now, and in the open clearing, she could see it frosting the ancient gray ruins and the open glade. She slowed to follow the road as it circled the stones and turned to come out the way she had come in. She was winning, and she meant to crow in triumph as she passed Prince Theodoric on the road back to the castle.

Anticipating that small pleasure made her smile.

However, when she did not pass him on the path

through the woods, she grew concerned, then worried.

The sky was darkened, and a sharp wind had picked up, blowing sheets of snow through the trees. Skeletal branches shook threateningly in the gusts as Ann passed. The grays shook their heads and blew steam through their nostrils. They could sense her unease; it was contagious.

"He's playing a trick," she thought, when she saw the curricle by the side of the road ahead, and she felt a stab of irritation. What kind of a fool did he take her for? she wondered.

She reined in her horses as she approached, ready to put on speed at the first sign of a trick.

But the chestnuts were slack in the harnesses, grazing unattended on a few stalks of winter grass, and as she approached, she saw the curricle was empty.

"Prince?" she called. "Your Highness?"

Her voice carried on the wind. The snow was picking up, coming down in small, sharp flakes, thick and fast. It was closing in now; she could barely see fifty feet ahead. The only sound was the wind sighing through the trees.

"Prince Theodoric, this is the most odious thing you've ever done!" she cried, exasperated. She brought her pair to a halt, peering around for some sign of life. She even looked upward, half expecting him to drop out of a tree, laughing at her. "I don't find this one bit amusing," she added, uncertainty had crept into her voice.

"Come now, you are making me uneasy!"

The gray on the left snorted and pawed the ground,

her eyes rolling back in her head, her ears flattened.
"Easy, Agnes," she said, but she felt anything but easy
herself. Arabella, on the right, picked up her sister's
fear and pawed at the ground. Ann reined them in
sternly. "Behave, both of you!" she commanded them.
"And you, too," she murmured to her heart, which
had begun to pound.

"Prince Theodoric! If you can hear me, make some
sound!" she cried.

Only the sound of snow sliding from a tree branch
answered her.

City bred, Ann felt distinctly unsettled here, alone
in the woods. She suddenly understood that nothing
she had learned at Miss Ridgely's had prepared her
for this. But that excellent preceptress had prepared
her students to be prepared for anything, and to face
the unknown with courage, so Ann swallowed, gathered up her skirts, and dismounted from the
phaeton.

"Prince Theodoric?" she called. Perhaps he had
been overtaken by a call of nature, and being a gentleman . . . or perhaps something worse had overtaken
him and he was even now lying helpless, somewhere
in the dark woods.

She looped her reins over a branch and bade her
grays to be good. Her boots sank in the snow, and she
slung the hem of her coat over her arm, tramping
across the road to look around.

The big chestnut geldings snorted and pawed at
the snow as she approached, and she noted that their
leads lay across the seat of the curricle, as if the
prince had thrown them there. She could not imagine

an emergency that would allow him to let the chestnuts stand for so long in the cold.

Carefully, she picked her way around the curricle
and peered into the woods. Looking down, she saw
blood, scarlet and glittering, as it lay in a trail of
droplets on the snow. It was fast being covered up.

Ann inhaled. Her urge was to run, to get into her
phaeton and get out of here, but she was a daughter
of David Ingersoll, and she straightened her shoulders, picked up her skirt, and followed the bright
droplets into the brush. Briars reached out and
gripped at her skirts, a branch like a skeletal hand dis-
lodged her bonnet, and she pushed it back impa-
tiently, peering into the gloom. "Prince Theodoric?"
she called.

A faint, guttural sound came from somewhere
deep ahead, and she plunged on, following the direction she thought it had come from.

"Prince?" she called.

He was crumpled in a heap beneath a bush, his
driving coat stained with crimson.

"Prince Theodoric!" Ann exclaimed, horrified. She
dropped to her knees in the snow and mud beside
him, gently touching his face.

He was, she noted, very pale, but hearing his
name, his eyes flickered open. "M-Miss Ingersoll," he
said, his breath frosting on the air. "Fancy meeting
you here." His lashes fluttered on his cheeks and he
muttered something in a language she did not understand. "It was supposed to be a joke, you know," he
said in English, and sighed.

"Prince Theodoric! You must not pass out," she

commanded brusquely. She shook his shoulder, and his head lolled. "What an odious joke," she said tersely.

Ann gazed distastefully at the spreading stain on his chest, and began to undo the big buttons. Tearing away his coat and waistcoat, she bit her underlip, as the stain spread starkly against his white shirt. "This is no joke," she whispered, pulling the buttons apart with trembling fingers, feeling his chest rise and fall in jerky breaths.

She pulled the pennant out of her sleeve and used it to dab at the blood. There was a gaping hole, she noted, and was relieved to see that no major organ seemed to have been damaged. Still, it was a nasty, messy business, and her best, she knew, would not be good enough without help, and help that must come soon.

Ann made up her mind; as much as she disliked leaving him here, she had no choice. She turned and ran back to the road, and with fumbling fingers set about unbuckling the harnesses that held her grays to the phaeton. When she had slipped them from the traces, she waved her bloodied pennant. "Go home!" she cried. "Shoo!"

The grays, tired and hungry, needed no further command. They took off at a brisk run, heading toward the stables at Coldstone Castle. She watched them disappear into the snow, hoping that they would find their way home and not wander. Here, at least, the weather would work with her.

She lifted Theo's head, and with some effort, managed to elevate his chest and shoulders, using her own body as a pillow.

"Prince," she called, "Can you hear me? What happened, can you tell me?"

His lashes, so dark against his pale skin, fluttered. "Shot again," he gasped, a grotesque imitation of laughter twisting his lips. "Came out of nowhere. Knocked me off balance. Went for cover . . . are they here?"

"Are who here? You must tell me what happened," Ann said, struggling to keep her voice calm and steady.

"Where are they? You should run, not stay here . . . I never thought to involve you, it was meant to be a joke . . . "

"You must stay awake!" Ann said. "This is no joke, Prince."

"It is a joke. A very bad joke, but a joke nonetheless," a voice said, and Ann looked up to see Randolph Rodney emerging from the woods.

"Randolph! Come help me! Someone has shot the prince!" Ann exclaimed.

Randolph shrugged. Slowly, he pushed his cloak back with his elbow and Ann saw the dull gleam of the pistol in his hand. He leveled it at her.

This is not happening, she thought, her heart sinking.

"Not you, Randolph," Theo said, struggling to sit up. "Oh, Lord, man, anyone but you."

"I am truly sorry, Theo," Randolph said almost gently. "But, yes, it is me."

"You took a shot at me in the park?"

"I'm sorry." Randolph inclined his head. The wind whipped his cloak around him. *He looks as if he's not there at all, as if he's a thousand miles away,* Ann thought. *And I feel the same way. This isn't happening.* But it was.

Slowly, Randolph took a few steps closer. "It was more than I could resist, you know," he said softly. "They offered me a great deal of money. You have no idea what it's like, not to have any money, not to have the woman you love because you can't afford to support her."

"Good God, Randolph! My best friend! After everything we've been through—" Theo broke off with a gasp of pain.

"You've killed men before, men you knew well. You know what it's like. I regret that I've become such a bad shot. Perhaps there is a part of me that still hesitates. I didn't think it would be so damned hard to kill you, but it is."

"You don't have to, Randolph. You really don't have to do this," Theo said.

My God, Ann thought, *he means to kill the prince. He means to kill us both.* Nothing in her experience had prepared her for this sort of emergency. She was having trouble accepting that this was happening at all.

"You're not sane, Randolph," she heard herself saying.

"No, my dear Ann, I am quite sane. I know what I want, and I know how to get it. When I come back, I shall tell them that I found you both dead here. Shot. Obviously you saw Theo in distress. Perhaps a poacher did it? Does that sound likely? I thought it would do."

"Randolph, I cannot believe this is you!" Ann said, growing irritated. "Theo is seriously wounded! He might bleed to death if we don't get some help soon!"

"Precisely the point, my dear Ann," the colonel replied with considerable sangfroid.

"Damn you, Randolph," Theo hissed, struggling to sit upright.

"I'll see you in hell, Theo," he replied with a faint smile. "And all the time, you thought it was that fool Johannes. Did you really think they would send a fop like him to do a man's errand? God, when you told me about your suspicions, about your little plot, this joke you wanted to play on Ann, it was all I could do not to laugh. You walked right into this trap. It's a great shame that Ann has to die, too, but—"

He brought out the pistol, leveling it at Ann's heart. "I have killed females before, you know. I will try to make it brief. Painless.

"If you understood how much I wanted Louisa, you would be happy to sacrifice yourself for it."

"You're not fit to marry Louisa," Ann snapped. She sniffled a little. "I don't want to die," she cried, bursting into tears.

"Oh, for God's sake, Ann, I thought better of you!" Randolph said, annoyed.

"Well, how would you feel? I mean I don't care about the prince, but I do care about me!" She reached into the sleeve of her riding coat. "Now look what you've done! You've made me cry, and my nose is running!"

The click, as Randolph cocked the pistol, was loud in the silence of the woods.

"My God, man!" Theo cried. He sat up, then fell back.

The pistol shot roared through the woods.

An odd look passed over Randolph's face.

He crumpled to the ground, a red stain spreading from a spot between his eyes, his laugh, horrible and wild, choked away as he fell and lay, lifeless, on the snow.

Startled, Theo twisted around to look at Ann.

The tiny pistol she had pulled from her sleeve was still smoking as it fell from her fingers.

"Good Lord!" she said softly. "When Miss Ridgely told me that if I were going to drive, I should carry a lady's pistol against highwaymen, I never thought— oh, I think I am going to faint!"

"Don't do that, please," Theo said.

"I *never* faint," Ann said, and promptly did so.

11

"*It was a tragedy,*" Prince Theodoric said, turning from the fire and moving his shoulder in its socket. The muscle still pained him in damp weather, and a summer squall had just passed over the mountains. "But at least I have the comfort of knowing that Colonel Rodney died trying to protect Miss Ingersoll and myself."

Ann, seated a little distance away from the fire, sighed. "I shall miss him very much. He was very brave." She kept her eyes firmly fastened on her fan, picking at the little gold tassel. This was one secret she would keep, and keep it forever.

"And you say that these brigands had been hired by certain traitors in Batavia to come to England and assassinate you," Mr. Ingersoll said, leaning back in his chair and frowning until his dark brows drew together over his nose. "By God, sir, that would have caused an international incident! Not to mention of course, what a tragedy your death would have been for your country, Prince." A servant moved forward to refill Mr. Ingersoll's glass. He sipped and nodded appreciatively. "And for ours. And you say they never caught the villains?"

"Never. As your daughter has told you, they were masked and cloaked. It all happened so suddenly . . . we were taken by surprise. Miss Ingersoll was very brave; she acted quickly and never lost her head. If it were not for her, I would be a dead man today, instead of those who plotted against the government." Prince Theodoric's voice was level; he met David Ingersoll's gaze with a bland look. "The magistrate rounded up some poachers and other well-known villains for my inspection, but I was able to safely say it was none of them. I suspect that they did their filthy deed and were out of the country within hours."

"You dealt with the traitors, the men who planned this?"

"Parliament tried them and passed their sentences. I had nothing to do with it. It was the will of the people. But today, you saw how our government works. It is similar to your English system, where everyone has a representative that they elect."

"Except females," Ann said dryly.

Theo threw up his hands in mock exasperation. "Give me time! I'm still trying to educate people in the manners of democracy! One radical idea at a time, please!" He suddenly smiled. He had been smiling a great deal lately, much more than he had in London. "Besides which, if you recall, today you received the Order of Batavia, first class, for your heroic efforts on behalf of the country. And a very nice ceremony to go with it!"

"Very true, and I am greatly honored," she said, glancing down at the gold and pearl sunburst pinned on her bodice. Ann inclined her head, but she smiled in return at Theo. "The only other medal I won was at Miss Ridgely's for marksmanship."

She accepted a glass of wine and looked about the drawing room of the Batavian Palace. It was, she decided, a comfortable, cheerful room. So far, almost everything she had seen about Batavia she had liked. The people were friendly, the climate this spring was warm and inviting. The little mountain principality, nestled among its vineyards, now in spring blossom, was beautiful. She could see why the prince loved it here.

Since she had not seen it when it had been stripped of its ancient furnishings by the Bonaparte cousin, she had no way of knowing how much effort Theo had invested in making certain that the residence was refurbished for the visit of his English friends.

As the prince and her father discussed that morning in Coldstone, she allowed her attention to drift away. She still had nightmares about that day. But as time passed, they grew dimmer.

Still, she could not find it in her heart to regret what she had done, nor the story she and Prince Theo had hastily pasted together to save the Coldstones from the disgrace of Randolph's actions. The Coldstones were so proud of their heroic cousin.

"Better to remember him as the man he was at his

finest, rather than what greed and ambition made him become," Theo said. "You can never understand what the war we fought can do to a man, how it can twist his soul inside him."

No, Ann could not. But she could and did understand how ambition, honed fine, could exclude every other feeling. No, this was their story and they stuck to it.

Anything else would have utterly destroyed Louisa, Ann thought, looking at her friend.

Louisa was not made of the sterner stuff of her own character. Her blood may not have been blue, but the steel that had forged David Ingersoll's fortunes still ran in his daughter's veins. Knowing what Randolph had been willing to do for love would have destroyed Louisa. As it was, she still wore a gentle air of grief that went well with the black mourning dress she was wearing tonight.

Ann studied Louisa, standing on the balcony looking out across the moonlit landscape. Louisa's heart, she knew, would heal. That was one of the reasons the duke and duchess had consented to allow her to accompany Ann and her father on this trip.

Did they still hope that the prince would propose? Ann wondered. Unlikely, she decided. The duke and duchess probably realized that gentlemen usually do not propose to daughters of the estate where they were almost murdered. Still, now that life could start up again, and there was no Randolph to impede the way, was there a possibility of sparks there? As far as Ann could tell, there seemed to be no lady in the prince's life; he was still determinedly as single as she was.

"Lady Louisa looks very becomingly in black," Johannes said at her elbow, and Ann looked up. Here, at least, was someone who would never change. Incorrigible, Johannes. And as always, completely and utterly charming.

His gaze followed Louisa on the balcony. "Yes, I think black becomes her very much with her fair hair and skin," he said thoughtfully. "You, of course, are always in looks," he added. "Even though I ought not to speak to you at all! How could you not encourage me when I was so very anxious to pay you court in London? It's too late now, you know, my heart is quite set upon Lady Louisa, and as soon as she begins to tire of being in love with a ghost, I shall be there."

Ann stared, openmouthed.

Johannes looked hurt. "I am a *completely* reformed rake, you know! I am now the most loyal citizen in the country! An upstanding citizen! No more ladies, no more cards, no more intrigue! No, really, it is true!" He put a hand on his heart. "Now that I have something to occupy my time, a place to use my talents, I have decided that nothing will do but that I must walk the, how do you say, straight and narrow. I think I shall even get married! My cousin has made me ambassador to Brazil. I am sure that I shall find an outlet for my talents for intrigue there! Do you think Lady Louisa would like Brazil? I must go and ask her at once! You know, my dear Miss Ingersoll, that fragile air of grieving gives her such a glow that I cannot resist!"

And with that, he walked out on the balcony, giving Louisa his most blinding smile.

It might just work, Ann thought, hugely amused. *She is a Coldstone and has a will of iron. If any female could keep Johannes in line, it would* have *to be Louisa.*

At that moment, Louisa smiled back at Johannes.

Watching the pair of them walk slowly down the balcony, Johannes delicately placing a hand on Louisa's arm as he pointed, with a sweeping gesture, toward the full moon hanging in the warm spring night, she smiled to herself. When he plucked a rose from a topiary growing in a pot, and presented it to Louisa with a flourish, Ann almost giggled, watching Louisa accept it.

Who knew? she thought. Anything can happen . . .

She felt someone looking at her, and glanced up to see Prince Theodoric. He was smiling his transforming smile as he rose and crossed the room toward her.

"I believe there is an expression that says a penny for your thoughts," he said.

Ann shook her head. "I doubt they are worth a penny," she replied.

Theo glanced at Mr. Ingersoll; he was jovially involved in a discussion with a buxom baroness, relict of a retired chancellor.

"Perhaps you would like to walk in the garden with me?" he asked, a little shyly. "I believe that the roses are just starting to bloom."

A little surprised, Ann agreed.

He offered her his arm, and they walked across the balcony and down a long flight of carved steps.

The garden was illuminated with stone lanterns, and populated with guests who strolled the gravel and admiring the late Princess Theodora's collection of roses, which was said to rival that of Malmaison, the Empress Josephine's residence outside Paris.

"I don't know much about flowers and suchlike," the prince said gruffly, "but they tell me this is one of the finest gardens in Europe!"

"It smells heavenly," Ann said. "In the morning, when I awaken, the first thing I can smell is the perfume of the flowers. It's a nice way to awaken."

"We have not had a chance to speak privately since you and your father arrived here, Miss Ingersoll. I hope that you have been enjoying your visit so far?"

"Oh, yes, Batavia is everything that you said it would be, and everyone has been most kind," she replied. "Did you command them to be so?" she could not resist adding.

"I am a head of state, not a dancing master," Theo said heavily, then, realizing that she was making a joke, he laughed, running his finger around the high collar of his tunic. "I particularly hoped that you would like Batavia and Batavia would like you."

"Then your hopes have been more than met," Ann replied. She reached out and touched a rose, running the open blossom through her fingers.

"No, my hopes have not been more than met. Not yet, Miss Ingersoll." Theo swallowed. "Ann!" he pronounced.

She looked up, eyebrows raised questioningly.

"You and I hold a great secret between us," he said.

"And the less said about that at this point, the better. What's done is done, and there is nothing we can do to change that. If you are worried that I will babble out the unhappy truth, you need have no qualms on that score," Ann told him seriously. "We have agreed that no purpose could be served by telling anyone the truth about Randolph. He has paid for his mistake, and I continue to pay for my actions. Even though I had no choice, it is not a pleasant thing to recall."

"You acted with extraordinary bravery. I owe you my life."

"I did what anyone would have done under the circumstances. At Miss Ridgely's school, we were taught to be able to meet any emergency."

Theo nodded. He frowned, gasping his hands behind his back and staring moodily out across the hills. "Ann!" he began again. "This isn't easy for me, you know! You should be helping me along here!"

"I would, if I knew what you were trying to say, Prince!"

"My friends call me Theo, you know," he said hopefully.

"Very well, then, Theo it shall be, in private, at least. But what are you trying to say, Theo?"

"When this all started, I really did believe that men were in every way superior to women." Theo swallowed hard, frowning. "Well, I was—I was—" he stopped, sputtered, and sighed. He took a deep breath. "I was wrong!" he finally said.

Ann burst into laughter. "You? Wrong? Never!" she cried, then changed her tone. "That is, thank you! I realize what that must have cost you." She sighed. "I have been wrong too. Not about the rights of women, but that men are stupid and inferior. Not all men are so."

"You have proved to me that females are as intelligent, as capable of action, and as shrewd in judgment as men," Theo pronounced. "By your own actions, you have changed a prejudice."

"And humbled my own pride," Ann acknowledged. "I think we have both been wrong. About our gender and about each other. What—what happened has brought out both the best and the worse in us."

"I hope that Mr. Briggs appreciates you. He is getting a fine female, a woman of discernment and intelligence and spirit," Theo said.

"What?" Ann asked blankly. She stopped dead in her tracks, puzzled. "What does Jeremy Briggs have to do with this?"

"He is, that is, I thought. Well, I mean, I walked in and he—you—were embracing! Aren't you?"

Ann pressed her hands to her cheeks. "Oh, no! I mean to say, well, it was the Duke of Cumberland all over again! Not Jeremy Briggs, that dried up twig of a man! All he is interested in is inheriting the business! Oh, no! Never! Ever! Twice in my life I have had to fend off unwanted attentions, and both times you would have to be there! Oh, no! Not Jeremy Briggs! Never!"

Prince Theo looked a little stunned. "You mean that you do not intend to marry that fellow?"

"Marry? Marry him? No, Theo, it is my intention never to marry! Why, I would sooner marry anyone, even you, than him!" Ann blurted out then, when she realized what she had said, she placed her hand over her mouth. "Oh, my wretched tongue! What an odious thing to say!" she cried, embarrassed. "But you know what I mean!"

"You mean that you would rather marry me than Mr. Briggs," the prince said gravely. Only a small muscle twitched in his jaw, betraying his grave expression.

"Oh!" Ann cried. "I am so sorry! I didn't mean that the way it sounded, you know."

"Oh, I think I understand. You do not intend to marry, but if you had to marry, you would prefer to marry me than to marry Mr. Briggs."

Ann shook her head, utterly confounded. "You know what I mean! We fight all the time! We never ever see eye to eye on anything! We are *always* at cross crabs!"

"Yes, an alliance between you and me would be completely out of the question," the prince agreed gravely. "Since you intend never to marry, and I of course, must."

"It would never work. Think of the difference in our ranks! You are royalty, I am a commoner. It would be a morganatic marriage! Out of the question!"

"Yes, you are quite right. Of course, you know, when your father becomes an Alderman, he will receive a knighthood! That would make you a peer's daughter, in a way, I think."

"A very dim sort of way. And when does Father plan to become an Alderman, pray tell?"

"Why, at the next term of the Lord Mayor. He's to be rewarded for his services to England, with this new trade treaty we've signed. You really ought to talk to your father once in a while, instead of gadding about the country in that phaeton of yours."

"I do not gad about the country!" Ann protested. "I knew something was in the works for Father, but I had no idea what! Anyway, this all just proves my point! We could never suit!"

"Yes, too true," Theo said sadly. "You see how we are quarreling right now! No doubt you would be such a shrew at the breakfast table that I would have to hide behind the newspaper."

"Shrew? Me?" Ann asked. "Fine words from an arrogant princeling!"

"Princeling? Princeling? You make me sound like someone in a fairy tale, who ought to be turned into a frog!"

"Well and so you should!"

They were both laughing.

Theo touched her cheek. "You know, if you kiss a frog, they say he will turn into a handsome prince," he teased.

"And will a handsome prince turn into a frog?" Ann asked, looking into his eyes. Her hand reached up to embrace his cheek.

"There's one way to find out," Theo replied, suiting his actions to his words.

Rebecca Baldwin lives and works on the
eastern shore of Maryland.

Let HarperMonogram Sweep You Away

SIREN'S SONG by Constance O'Banyon
Over Seven Million Copies of Her Books Are in Print!
Beautiful Dominique Charbonneau is determined to free her brother, even if it means becoming a stowaway aboard Judah Gallant's pirate ship. But Gallant is not the rogue he appears, and Dominique is torn between duty and a love she might never know again.

THE AUTUMN LORD by Susan Sizemore
A Time Travel Romance
Truth is stranger than fiction when '90s woman Diane Teal is transported back to medieval France and must rely on the protection of Baron Simon de Argent. She finds herself unable to communicate except when telling stories. Fortunately she and Simone both speak the language of love.

GHOST OF MY DREAMS by Angie Ray
RITA and Golden Heart Award-winning Author
Miss Mary Goodwin refuses to believe her fiancé's warnings that Helsbury House is haunted—until the deceased Earl appears. Will the passion of two young lovers overcome the ghost, or is he actually a bit of a romantic himself?

A ROYAL VISIT by Rebecca Baldwin
An affair of state becomes an affair of the heart when Prince Theodoric of Batavia travels to England to find a bride. He is looking for a titled lady, but a resourceful and charming merchant's daughter shows him that love can be found where one least expects it.

And in case you missed last month's selections...
KISS ME, KATIE by Robin Lee Hatcher
Bestselling Author
When high-spirited suffragette Katie Jones takes a job at a local Idaho newspaper with her childhood friend, Benjamin Rafferty, she never expects love to be the top story. A warm and touching romance from one of the most beloved Americana writers.